SECOND CHANCE RANCH

Montana, book 5

RJ SCOTT

Love Lane Books

Second Chance Ranch

Montana series, book 5

Copyright ©2018 RJ Scott

Cover design by Meredith Russell, Edited by Sue Laybourn

Published by Love Lane Books Limited

ISBN 978-1725973879

All Rights Reserved

Dedication

With thanks to my editor Sue, who put the hours in, my beta Elin for her wisdom, and my army of proofers. Love you all.

And always for my family.

RJ SCOTT

Montana 5

SECOND CHANCE Ranch

Chapter One

ROB BRADY KNEW THREE THINGS. HIS SISTER WAS DEAD, HE was the guardian to her two boys, and he was stuck in Hell.

And why am I fixating on Hell?

Oh yeah, the room, the kids, the crushing grief of absolutely fucking *everything.*

If Hell was a small, airless room with no windows, a flickering light, and two utterly silent children staring at him as if he'd personally murdered their mother.

Oh, and a thin-lipped woman from Child Protection Services looking at him the same way.

Of course, he hadn't killed his sister because he only *ever* took out the bad guys. With ruthless efficiency, he'd carved out the poison in the US and kept its citizens safe. Most people would've described him as an assassin, but he was more than that; the last resort when normal lines of defense failed.

At least, he used to be until he caught a bullet things went pear-shaped.

"How long have they been on their own?" Rob Brady

didn't know what else to ask. He wanted to be angry with the DCFS but how could he be? Instead, he wavered between anger and guilt, and it was guilt that was winning.

"Mr. Brady, they were never on their own."

"My sister—" He stopped talking when he realized he was just about to state how long ago his sister died when her children were sitting right there in the room. Lowering his tone, he then turned to Sylvia from the DCFS, efficient and steady, and just ever so slightly pissed at him. "A year. They've been on their own a year."

Sylvia inhaled sharply and clutched her folders to her chest.

"And for a little less than that, we have tried to track down their uncle and been unable to find anything."

"I know. I get that." Anyone trying to find him would reach several dead-ends whichever way they went. First of all the navy and his time in the SEALs, then when he joined the team combatting mainland terrorism. At every turn, his existence was classified, and in the end, he'd become nothing more than a ghost. "That isn't my point."

Sylvia tapped a finger on the files in a steady rhythm. "Then please, can you enlighten me as to what exactly *is* your point?"

He opened the door and gestured for her to go into the hallway, following her out and shutting it behind them. He had questions and didn't want to ask them in front of his nephews.

"Why has no one adopted them? Why don't they have a forever home with a new family?"

"Because your sister's intention was that you would take the boys. It's explicitly stated in every legal form we have, and it was her dying wish."

"But she couldn't have known I would ever come back.

Or that I was even alive..." He floundered for something to say. He'd come back to town on the off chance he'd see what was left of his extended family from a distance, and instead, he'd learned his sister was dead, after losing a battle with cancer, that there was no father in the picture, and that his nephews were *in the system.*

"Nonetheless, they are legally your responsibility. Given you worked so hard to get authorization from Governor Chilton, something I've never seen before, along with psych evals that no normal person would have access to, you are now in a position to leave with your nephews."

The minute he'd heard about the boys, he'd realized he needed to get things done. He'd called in favors, had people who owed him create a backstory so tight he seemed like Mother fucking Teresa, and now he was here. His nephews needed a home, and he thought on his feet because he only had another three good months to put anything in place for them. He wanted them looked after, safe, and so he had one more mission before leaving. He'd have to delay spending his last weeks on a beach in Aruba, sipping cocktails and sleeping with anything that moved.

"I can take them today?" he asked. A small, hesitant part of him wanted her to say no, that there were more details to be ironed out.

"Yes."

"Now?"

"Yes." She pursed her lips as if it were against her better judgment. But he'd passed all the checks, and the references were sound, he had the governor's endorsement. It was done.

"Okay then."

He pushed back into the room. Bran, the older of his two nephews, stared at him steadily. Toby, the youngest, sniffled and gripped his brother hard. Any ordinary uncle would've hugged them close and told them everything was going to be okay. But he wasn't a regular uncle, and he swore Bran knew that because there was accusation in his eyes.

You don't even know us; he seemed to be saying.

Was it right for Rob to be taking them from their new foster home? They'd been placed with a family currently fostering six kids, and on the surface, everything seemed okay. He'd done his due diligence, and the parents checked out, but there was a weird vibe in the house, a rule of fear, and he didn't like it.

He'd stayed alive this long by listening to his instinct, and his gut told him he should take Bran and Toby, that he was the boys' kin. He also knew where he could find them a better home. In the mountains, with rivers and horses, and a whole group of people who would look out for them.

"Everything will be okay." Was he reassuring himself or the boys?

If anyone who knew him had seen he was being handed two children to take care of, they'd call the cops.

Of course, he could handle the cops. He'd done it before, but the kids would slow him down. Unless he strapped them to his back and—

"Mr. Brady?"

Sylvia talked to him, or at him, and from her expression, she wasn't impressed he'd stopped listening.

"Sorry, say again?" He glanced at Toby who was sniffling harder and snuggling deeper into his brother. *I should go to Toby and...*

And what?

Do what? Say what? Scare the kid rigid by being all up in his face?

"We need an address for our records. Unless you reside with Governor Chilton?" The last she added sarcastically.

Oh yeah, a house, an address, he probably needed those. He'd managed to fool them with his credentials so far, and the recommendation he'd gotten from the governor for a favor owed had cut through the red tape. The address was easy; it was the only place he had on his to-do list, the one where the kids could maybe have a home. He just needed to hire a lawyer, update his will, get Justin to agree to his proposal, and he'd be able to leave without any worries.

"Crooked Tree Ranch, outside of Helena, Montana."

She dutifully filled it in.

"And a phone number?"

He gave her his private cell number.

"Okay then," he said enthusiastically, causing Toby to jump a mile.

Bran immediately gripped his brother's hand and sent Rob as much of a condemning look as an eight-year-old could muster.

"Sorry," he apologized, meeting the stern gaze of a not-at-all-amused Sylvia. He gave her his best smile, the one that got him into the beds of men and women all over the continental US. She didn't smile back or thaw in any way. Maybe he was losing his skills.

Probably a side effect of lead leaking from the fragments of the bullet lodged in his thoracic vertebrae.

"Come on kids." He stood, and the boys, holding hands, left the room first. He followed, but as he was about to walk past the caseworker, she stopped him, and he found himself under the scrutiny of her dark gray eyes.

"Tell me what you're doing now," she demanded and then softened it with a, "please."

He could've lied his way out of there, he could've tried to charm her, but she cared for the kids she had on her books and needed him to be entirely honest, and that was something he'd forgotten how to be. So he spoke from the same heart that wouldn't turn away his flesh and blood, despite the world of limited possibilities he was trying to live in.

"Bran and Toby are my family; I will protect them for as long as I live."

Okay, so that was a bit melodramatic, but sue him. It felt as if the occasion called for it, and he wasn't lying. No one was getting past him to the kids. Not bullies or the authorities or even political assassins. Not while he could still stand, anyway.

She squeezed his arm, and he waited for more questions, but she released him. "You will be contacted by a local office near you. Welfare checks, not even you can avoid."

"I'll welcome them," he murmured.

She dropped her hold. "Okay," she said and then watched them as Rob gathered up his new family and left.

He'd bought everything Sylvia had said he needed to get. She'd given him the list a week ago when he'd first found out what had happened. Everything was crammed into his brand-new SUV. He'd handed over a credit card at a store and told them to go mad. There was the correct size booster seat for Toby, along with numerous bags of things that the lady told him boys of eight and five would need. Everything except clothes because she didn't know their sizes, and Rob couldn't give her those. The bill was massive, but he felt more in control knowing he'd ticked all that off the list.

Of course, Bran and Toby had their belongings. Not too much, but a couple of boxes and a small suitcase each. Toby carried a ratty old bunny around with him on a permanent basis, and Bran kept telling him he needed to take good care of it. Bran didn't appear to have anything he needed to keep hold of. Except for his little brother of course.

Rob helped strap them in, tested everything twice, then

surrounded them with the softer things like blankets and boxes because there was absolutely no room for it all in the trunk. Then he shut their doors, climbed into the driver's seat, and locked them all in.

Habit.

His stomach rumbled. He hadn't eaten since last night, and even though he was sure the kids had eaten breakfast somewhere, he decided it was his duty to keep them fed.

"So, Bran, Toby, are you hungry?"

Toby hid his face in his bunny, and Bran answered for both of them.

"We're both hungry, Uncle Rob."

"McDonald's?" he suggested, which got Toby to peer from around the rabbit. "I know it's not the healthiest food, and I should find you vegetables or something, but that can wait, right? A road trip deserves McDonald's. Am I right?" He was rambling, and Bran stared at him with what he was sure was disapproval and disappointment.

He turned back to face the front, holding the steering wheel so tight his knuckles whitened.

He'd stared down death.

Hell, he'd *been* death.

Keeping his country safe had meant he'd been in situations that others would run screaming from, but he couldn't face the disillusionment in one little boy's eyes.

He was so fucked.

———

THEY REACHED the edge of Crooked Tree land in the dark, after a solid day of driving, and Rob deliberately stopped at a gas station on the edge of town, so that they could all take a comfort break.

It was a little after eight in the evening, no more than five miles from the ranch, and he was so close he could taste the fear in him that Justin would send the three of them away.

He needed to make a small amount of time for himself to formulate a proper plan, as opposed to the one he was using right now. This mostly consisted of running to Justin and hoping for the best.

"Cute kids," a woman with dark curly hair said to him in the queue, all kinds of friendly and smiling. He was probably supposed to say something back to her; objectively he knew that. So he channeled one of his undercover personas and became a man acceptable to socialize with.

"Thanks."

That was the wrong move because it opened the floodgates for this very proud momma. "I remember when my Jillian was that age, and now we're driving through the night all over the country visiting colleges. Time flies so fast."

"I know."

"Enjoy them this age while you can," she added, then smiled at him again and finished paying. He felt himself smile in return and thought that if he'd been in front of a mirror, his lips would've curved into something more innocent than blank-faced suspicion. He even congratulated himself for acting normal enough that he hadn't scared the shit out of her as he grabbed random snacks, probably unhealthy ones, with high levels of fats and god-knew-what kinds of colorants. Along with cereal bars and cartons of orange juice because that was healthy for kids, right?

They'd eaten at drive-throughs the last day, journeyed through the night, with short breaks like this one, and he'd driven straight to Montana. He'd been so damn tired when he reached Helena but energized when he realized he was so close to a bed and maybe a real meal.

And somewhere the boys might one day call home.

His back ached like a bitch. Over-the-counter meds had taken the edge off, but he held back on the Fentanyl as he was driving. That was for when he was in his room and only had himself to consider.

Listening to the curly-haired woman had seemed so normal. The kids deserved better than an Uncle who didn't have a freaking clue what he was doing. They deserved someone like her or Justin and his Sam or maybe one of the other families at Crooked Tree. Family and safety. Crooked Tree had all of that. He'd seen it. Brothers, sisters, family, friends; it was like some goddamned *Little House on the Prairie*. Only in the mountains. By the Blackfoot River.

And not on a prairie at all.

Justin would give him and the kids somewhere to sleep. He was sure of it. There was no way he would turn them away, right?

With the kids strapped back in the car and Toby looking as if he was dozing off, Rob pulled his cell phone out, intent on calling Justin, giving him a heads-up. It seemed only right that he offered at least that level of politeness. The curly-haired woman gave him a wave and climbed into the backseat of an old car, buckling up and leaning forward to talk to her husband or daughter, or whoever it was driving.

The car pulled forward, indicating to turn right, the opposite way to where he and the kids would be going. In that car was a normal family, doing normal things.

He was almost envious.

Then, right in front of his SUV, a semi hurtled out of nowhere and rammed into their car waiting to turn onto the main road. The world exploded into a chaos of fire and trapped civilians. Cursing, he reversed the SUV away from the carnage, parking it well back. Then instinct and adrenaline kicked in.

He didn't hesitate to run toward the twisted burning wreckage.

Chapter Two

"YOUR BROTHER IS ON LINE ONE!" GRACE CALLED THROUGH the open doorway.

Aaron sighed and turned to face her, not wanting to talk to any brother who was going to mess with him getting off shift on time. He had ten minutes to go, and then freedom. Not that he hated his job. That wasn't an issue. He'd been an EMT here for six years now, and the slower pace suited his goals for the rest of his life. Peace. Quiet. Family. It's what he'd promised himself when he'd left the Army, and so far everything was on track.

Until his brother's wife got pregnant. She was due in three weeks, and Eddie was freaking the hell out. Which was stupid, given he'd already been through the new baby thing twice with Milly and Jake.

"Which brother?"

Please let it just be Saul organizing a dinner, or Jason wanting to meet up for a beer, or Ryan wanting to catch up about last week's EMT crossover with his team at the sheriff's station. As long as it's not Eddie. Please, not Eddie, with his awkward questions about things no brothers should discuss over Sunday dinner.

"I'm not your answering service," Grace snapped before vanishing into their bus which they were cleaning down from the last run.

Great. A brother and *a pissy Grace.* He went to the phone, pressed the flashing button, and forced himself not to sound at all irritated. It didn't work.

"I have ten minutes to the end of my shift," he warned whichever brother this was. "And I'm due at Hepburn House."

Ordinarily, that would be enough to get his brothers to back off. Hepburn House was a private place just outside of town, for veterans like him who'd seen too much and needed some space to readjust to civilian life. They respected his need to be involved in something so supportive, and never asked a single question about his time overseas.

That didn't mean they wouldn't listen to him on a bad day, but mostly they left his past where he needed it to stay.

"No worries," Saul replied, and Aaron heaved a sigh of relief. Saul, he could handle. "I was making sure you're going to be here Sunday. Jordan and his brother are here, and I'm just ticking the boxes."

"Of course." He could have added that he was always there. Every Sunday he'd made it to dinner. Sometimes, if he was on shift, there was only enough time to pick up a bag of food from whatever was left, but he always tried.

All his brothers attended, because Saul was the head of the family and had spent his entire life keeping them together, and every one of the remaining four brothers respected that.

"Good. Stay safe."

Saul ended every phone call with those words, always the

worrier. That was why they loved him so much, given he'd been both Mom and Dad to them all since he was eighteen.

"Always."

Glancing at his watch, he saw he had only five minutes left, so he went to help Grace with finishing the bus duties.

Which is when he found her up on a stool as it wobbled and nearly deposited her on the floor.

"What the hell?" he demanded, setting her carefully on the ground, then dropping the new supplies next to her. "Grace Mya Davies, I told you to call me," he added, and she winced up at him.

"I'm not useless," she snapped, and tears collected in her eyes.

Oh god, no. Not emotion. He could handle blood, gore, amputations, war, even his brother's kids after they'd had soda laced with colorants, but when Grace cried, it was game over. He pulled her in for a hug, holding her carefully. Pregnant women surrounded him. Or at least two, his sister-in-law and his partner.

"Not useless," he murmured. "Just four months pregnant and very short. Which is why you let me reach the top shelves, and you don't climb on the stool to get to things."

She nodded against his shirt, which felt damp. "I'm not that short."

He wasn't unusually tall, a solid six foot, but at five one she was and always would be shorter than him by a mile.

"Leslie says I should stop working," she murmured.

"She would say that. She's your sister, and she's worried about you."

"Stupid crying." Her tone changed to one of self-recrimination, and he squeezed her tight and then let her go. Grace Davies was a spitfire as well as being a focused serious professional, and being pregnant was messing with her head.

"I could go for a coffee after shift," he suggested. "I've got some time if you want in with a hot chocolate?"

She pulled away from him and shook her head, not even meeting his gaze. She'd done this a lot recently, and he put it down to hormones because he really couldn't think of another reason. They were friends, and he could only guess that it was something to do with his stupid question four weeks back about who the father of her baby was. Things hadn't gotten back to normal yet.

Me and my big mouth.

The emergency announcement was loud, startling him and Grace, even though they were used to it; RTA at the Ester Gas Station on Pine Ridge Road. It didn't matter that they were only one minute from the end of the shift. A call was a call, and they were both ready to go.

They were leaving the hospital within a few seconds and reached Pine Ridge in less than five minutes. Firefighters were already on the scene, the scarlet engines blocking the road and only allowing a small space for the EMTs to get through. Aaron spotted his brother Jason immediately but bypassed him and quickly crossed to the crushed metal of what remained of an SUV, pinned to a gas pump by a semi.

"Stay back," Jason shouted, reached for him, and yanked at his arm, stopping him from getting closer. "We have a fire near the main fuel tanks." Jason was his brother, but he was also controlling the scene, and Aaron knew it was Jason who would have answers.

"Talk to me," Aaron demanded.

He could see enough; a semi had lost control coming down this side of the mountain, crashing into a car waiting to turn onto the main road, pushing it into the gas pumps. They were lucky they weren't attending a conflagration where everyone was dead already.

Where there is life, it's my job to bring hope.

"Semi driver out, not a scratch, family in the compact trapped. A further civilian in the car who won't get the hell out."

Aaron scanned the area, checking for ingress. The driver of the semi was standing by his truck, pale and shaky, covered in blood, but walking. They were the first EMTs on the scene. He assessed the situation and pressed a hand to Grace's shoulder. There was no way into the twisted, mangled metal except for climbing, and he was taking point on this.

"I'm going to look." He motioned for Grace to move back and away. At first, she stubbornly stood there, and he waited until it hit her she had the baby to think about and didn't *need* to get involved yet.

"Aaron, stay back," Jason ordered, right up in his face and gripping his arm. "Suppressing this fire is going to take time."

Aaron shrugged him off. "I'm not watching people burn to death." The words "little brother, try to stop me" remained unspoken.

Shouting cut through their seconds-long standoff, ordering to get closer and kill the fire. Then Jason finally released his hold.

"Don't you fucking die."

He was away before his brother had a chance to stop him, scrambling over the back of the car, peering through the sunroof, and assessing what he could see.

A woman lay awkwardly on the back seat, pinned by the seatbelt, blood from a wound on the side of her head matting her dark curly hair. Her eyes were open, and he reached through and checked her pulse. Visually she looked like she'd walk away from this, but only tests would tell what had happened inside her. For a moment she was confused, and then she gasped.

"Lewis, Alana."

Two names. Two more souls inside the car.

Jason crawled in behind him, and between him and another firefighter the woman was removed, and that just left the other two, designated in his head as Driver and Passenger Two.

He couldn't see a way into the front; there was no gap big enough for him to get through, and what was there was crushed and mingled with the semi.

"Paramedics!" A man called, forceful and demanding. Evidently, the civilian who had taken it upon himself to climb into this death trap. "Bleeding out."

Aaron peered through the only space he had, saw one hell of a lot of blood and not much more.

"Paramedic. I can't get to you."

"Wait," the voice said, and then the seat on the right moved, and in a scramble of limbs, a terrified teenager pushed through or was shoved through. At first glance, she seemed fine, untouched, and Aaron had seen that before in crashes like this where, by some miracle, a passenger was entirely unharmed.

"Mom," the girl cried, crawling past him and stumbling to where her mom was on a gurney being pushed away.

"Quick," the man called, and a hand came through and gripped Aaron's shirt, blood slick on his fingers.

Aaron slid through the space vacated by the daughter and assessed the scene with speed and the necessary dispassion.

A driver, bleeding, neck wound, and a man crouching awkwardly over him like the specter of death, his fingers pressed to a gash in the driver's neck. Aaron couldn't see the man's face, but he heard him well enough.

"Penetrating neck injury. Conscious and alert on arrival. Continuous blood loss," the man reported, staccato and clear. "We need to get this bleeding stopped."

Aaron glanced behind him. There was immediate asphyxia and hemorrhagic risk, and they had to move fast. "We're pinned in." He wriggled again to get closer; his bag stuck awkwardly until he managed to yank it through. The roar of blades cutting metal filled the cramped space. Jason and his fellow firefighters were attempting to get them free.

"Tell me you have a hemostatic dressing in there." The man shifted a little to give Aaron another chance of getting even closer. He had a neat beard, dark hair, and a steady, focused precision to his movements.

Of course, Aaron had a hemostatic dressing. Even if he'd had to fund it himself, he'd have the lifesaving bandages in his kit. One-handed, he grabbed the packet and shimmied back, pressed hard against the stranger holding his hand over the driver's neck. He ripped open the package, using a combination of his only free hand and his teeth and winced as it spilled out.

"On three," Aaron ordered. "One, two, three."

The man moved his hand, and Aaron applied the bandage to the gash, holding it firm, watching as blood spilled out of the side of it and then slowly stopped. With the immediate danger of bleeding out from the neck wound averted, Aaron carried out as many checks as he could.

"Get out now," he ordered the other man. This was a dangerous situation. There was fire, and the smell of gas was all around them. This car could go up in flames at any moment, and the last thing he needed was an extra civilian on his watch.

The man was conflicted. Aaron could see it in his expression and the way he glanced over his shoulder and then back at Aaron. But the conflict died immediately, and he was completely focused.

"Staying."

"Don't be stupid. Get out now."

The man shook his head. "I'm holding him still."

"It's dangerous."

"Not moving until we get someone in here backing you up."

"I don't need you here," Aaron snapped, but the man wasn't shifting at all.

"Noted," was the stranger's reply.

He had that same stubbornness in his expression he'd seen so many times in the war. *No man is left to die alone.*

"Stubborn fucker," Aaron announced, narrowing his focus when the man winked at him.

Winked at him. Arrogant asshole.

"Always," he murmured.

Aaron had seen his share of idiot heroics, and the expression on this imbecile's face was one he recognized. It was unshakeable belief that he was indestructible, that nothing could hurt him. That was how people died. This man was forces-trained the same as he was.

Like recognized like.

So Aaron went for an order instead of a request. "Get the fuck out of the car, soldier." Something snapped and crackled above their head, and the car heaved to the left.

"Sailor, and no."

The car moved again, the space getting smaller, and Mr. Navy shifted his position, using his back to push up on the crushed metal, holding it steady. Goddamned idiot. Probably some freaking Navy SEAL, just waiting to get himself killed.

"Last time someone insisted on staying with me against orders, a bullet tore an artery, and he bled out in seconds."

"That's life."

"I'm ordering you to get the hell out."

"I probably outrank you."

"Fuck you, Navy," Aaron snapped, aware this was not a fight he was going to win.

"Fuck you right back, Army."

They stared at each other. The chaos of noise as the jaws of life wrenched at metal stole any more chances of talking, and the space over their heads increased a little. Navy had dark green eyes and the focused determination of someone who'd seen war and learned not to show fear. There was a fire in their depths, and yeah, between them, they were supporting the driver's head and neck. With both of them, there was a chance this guy could get out of this alive.

So they stared and waited, and it seemed like a lifetime of memories passed between them.

I've seen things. I've known war. I've held a man as he died.

The car roof shifted again, no longer pressing against Navy, and Aaron saw the relief in Navy's eyes the moment the pressure lifted.

Then Jason was giving orders, dictating to his men how to maneuver the patient out of the wreckage.

"Get out of here," Jason told Navy. "We've got this."

Only when Jason and another firefighter had the guy onto the backboard did Navy leave, with a final nod as if he was clearing the situation.

Aaron used his feet to push back, and Jason helped him out, moving immediately into the space Aaron had just vacated. Here was where the firefighters took over to get the driver and backboard out and then onto the nearest emergency room, which was in Helena. He clambered up and out, but there was no sign of Navy.

"You okay?" Grace asked, patting him and checking for injury.

"The blood isn't mine," Aaron murmured.

They didn't talk about the chances of the driver making it out alive. They just got him into the bus and headed from the scene in the direction of Helena. He drove, and Grace was in the back monitoring vitals, the wife, and daughter of the driver with her. As they left, he looked at the wreckage. The tangled semi was half in the road, and just beyond it, the fire trucks and an SUV, with Navy next to it watching them leave.

Aaron raised a hand in acknowledgment as they passed, and Navy nodded.

I wonder what your story is.

Chapter Three

ROB HAD WANTED TO STAY IN THE CAR WITH THE PARAMEDIC and the guy bleeding out, trying to save him, wanting to make a difference. The whole time, he hadn't even considered the kids in the car. He'd blindly switched into control mode and held the driver's life in his hands. That was what he was trained to do. Way before he killed people for a living, he'd been a SEAL. He'd performed miracles under fire, been the hero the US needed him to be, just as he'd been right here in the middle of Montana. But he'd been ordered to leave the car, and the moment the EMT told him that, he'd rebelled. No one told him what to do. He had lives to save, and he wasn't going anywhere.

It didn't matter that his back was in spasm and the pain was stealing his breath, or that his vision was blurry, or even that, for a moment in the car, he couldn't remember what to do to help the injured man.

It only hit him when he clambered out of the car, helped out by a firefighter who'd cursed him for his stupidity. Why had he done that? Why had he put a stranger first, and why the hell had he decided it was vital he stay in the damn car?

See, this is why I'm not fit to be any kind of guardian to them.

Rob was obligated to deal with an issue he should never have had to face. The children in his SUV, his nephews, had to get to a family, a *real* one, and not stay with their fucked-up uncle. But he couldn't get them situated if he were dead.

He was a trained killer, and because of that, his keen sense of self-preservation didn't extend beyond himself. Sometimes it was only that which kept him alive. Justin used to accuse him of being emotionally detached, and fucked up. What would Justin's opinion be now if he was watching this confusion he was dealing with.

On the one hand saving the lives of strangers.

On the other looking out for his nephews.

I needed to leave them. I will always put danger and adrenaline above what is left of my family. Because that is the kind of fucked-up brain I have.

"Sir? Can I ask a few questions?"

The voice took him by surprise, and he startled, spinning on his heel to face a new threat, his hand instinctively reaching for a weapon.

He saw the flash of shock in the sheriff's face, his instant reaction of going for his own weapon, and the relaxed stance he moved into when Rob held his hands out in front of him.

I'm not a threat to you. He hoped that was the message he was conveying. Hell, he'd been shot for a lot less than being caught by surprise and reacting badly. There was absolutely no reason why he would want to detain Rob, but already he was on the balls of his feet ready to run. *Stupid.*

"My bad," he apologized.

The sheriff inclined his head but remained cautious as he held out a hand. "Sheriff Ryan Carter. Ryan."

"Robert Brady. Rob." They shook hands, and then the

sheriff gestured that they move away from the accident, which took them closer to Rob's car and the children inside. At least he could check on them. *Why didn't you do that before? They're important.* Damn it. Just another mark in the no-way-am-I-fit-to-be-a-dad column.

"Are you armed, Mr. Brady?"

Rob guessed the sheriff needed to ask after he'd just tried to defend himself in a knee-jerk reaction. Any cop worth their salt would have seen the gesture and read it for what it was. He needed to work on not automatically reaching for his gun whenever he was startled. He wasn't ready to die because of his stupidity. Well, not yet anyway.

"No, sir. It's in a static lockbox in the car, and I have all the correct permits."

"Law enforcement?"

"Civilian security." The lie was quick now and so easy, and he'd said it so often it had become the truth of what he did. The sheriff didn't immediately ask for the permits, but Rob guessed at some point in this conversation it would come up, so he pulled everything out, carefully, and handed it all over.

The sheriff called in the details, as Rob assumed he would, then returned the papers to him.

"Can you fill in some details for me about what you witnessed?"

Now that he could do. He just had to attempt to recall everything, push past a migraine and the pain, and focus on the details.

"The semi lost control coming over the top of the hill. The car in front of me was indicating to turn onto the highway. The semi had no chance to avoid the car when it slid on gravel and came directly for the gas station." He pressed his fingers to his temples and massaged the pressure point there.

"Are you hurt, sir?" the sheriff asked.

"No, it's just..." he didn't finish and instead focused on the *situation*. "It was a hard collision. I reversed my vehicle away from the gas pumps and the fire and then used an available ingress to reach the driver. Mom and daughter were conscious and alert, but the driver was non-responsive, neck injury, and potential internal trauma."

"Had the car pulled onto the highway?"

"No, the car was still behind the line. The semi sideswiped, but it could have been worse."

"Sir, do you need medical attention?"

Rob frowned. He was okay. He'd stopped rubbing his temples, and it wasn't him that was hurt, but the sheriff was gesturing at his shirt. When Rob looked down, he saw bloodstains in patches on the front of his shirt and his right sleeve. Not only that, but his hands were itchy with it, even though he hadn't noticed before. He wiped his hand on his jeans and shrugged.

"No, I'm not injured."

"I need your address for our records so I can get a full statement as a primary witness."

Years of deep-seated anonymity made Rob pause, but who cared what he was called or where he lived. He wasn't the man he'd been before. He was just an uncle with limited time and a family to make for his nephews. He was *nothing* now.

"I'm between places, but I'm staying with friends at Crooked Tree Ranch from tonight. Justin Allens."

As long as Justin doesn't shoot me on sight.

The sheriff didn't appear to think that was weird, merely

wrote what Rob had said, and nodded. "Are you available to come to the station tomorrow?"

"Actually, I've been driving solid for more than a day, and the kids are exhausted. Can I call the office and make an appointment?"

Hell, he'd made himself sound like he was a responsible adult there. Go figure. It wasn't that he was trying to avoid talking to the sheriff, but he had a purpose and talking to local law enforcement wasn't part of the plan.

Actually the start of the plan was simply. Get to Crooked Tree. Persuade Justin not to kill him. The rest would follow.

"It's not a problem, I'll take a drive out to Crooked Tree in the morning." The sheriff closed his notebook. "You planning on staying long there?"

Sheriff Ryan was making conversation but Rob bit back the instinct to inquire why the hell he thought that was an okay question to ask.

Evasion was ingrained in every inch of him so *no one* needed to know his movements.

"I need to get the kids to the ranch." He waved at his car, and the sheriff glanced from him to the car and back. "But we'll be there for a while. A week minimum." *Unless I can dump and run faster than that.* He was coming over as cagey, and he knew a hell of a lot better than that. *Act natural.*

"Hmm." Sheriff Carter hooked his thumbs in his belt. "It's a nice place for a vacation."

The man was fishing. Rob could hear it in his tone.

"It's not just a vacation. Justin is a friend, from work."

The sheriff straightened, and his narrow focus turned to something more thoughtful. He didn't ask any further questions though, as the fire chief had appeared at his elbow. Rob backed away to the car before he was asked anything else. Usually, he'd deal with this, have a backstory, but it seemed as though telling the truth after all these years was something he couldn't handle.

He took one last look at the accident scene. The potential fire was under control, and he watched the firefighters pulling the two vehicles apart. He hoped the little family was okay.

He'd known that Bran and Toby would be out of range of the fire. Then he left them with a shouted, "Stay here," and climbed mindlessly, fearlessly, into the burning car.

I left them.

Rob didn't know what was worse. That he'd left them to put his life in danger? That they'd seen him do that? That he was getting back into his car with blood on his clothes? Or, maybe, that in reality the kids were sitting silently waiting for him.

Shouldn't they be irritated with him or scared of the fire or angry or excited or *something*? Why weren't they showing any emotion at all? They were sitting exactly where he'd left them when the accident had happened. In fact, the only sign that they'd moved was the empty chip packet on Toby's lap, which showed that he had at least eaten the last of the snacks from back in Helena.

"You okay?" Rob asked, twisting in his seat to check on them.

Bran side-eyed Toby and then nodded.

"Is everyone in the car okay?" Bran asked, his tone quiet.

"Yep." He didn't want to talk about the accident or the injuries or anything like that.

"I bet if you'd been there when mom was dying you could have saved her," Bran pointed out. His tone was flat, and he wasn't accusing, just stating fact. "She always said you were a hero."

"A hero," Toby murmured after his brother.

Rob's chest tightened. He'd seen her medical records;

there was nothing he could have done. No transplant, or donation from him would have fixed the cancer that killed her.

You could have been there to hold her hand though.

"You ready to go see the horses at the ranch?" Rob changed the subject and faced the front before either boy answered. It didn't matter what they said, because the three of them were going to Crooked Tree, and that's where the horses were.

Rob told himself that Justin would welcome him and the kids. But when he pulled up at the Crooked Tree Ranch turn, he'd gone from convinced he'd be welcome to thinking Justin would get a gun and shoot him.

Well, that would solve the issue of the alternative slow, painful death, I guess.

He parked and went to the trunk, pulled off the bloody shirt and wiped himself as best as he could, putting on a new one and smoothing the wrinkled material. The road to the ranch was long, a smooth bend ending at a parking area. He recognized the layout. After all, he'd been here before, in the dead of night with no witnesses except Justin. The parking area had more lighting now, and he drove up and under the first of the lights, closest to the exit, reversing into a space.

Just in case.

"We're here," he announced. Should he leave the kids in the car again? Go and find Justin himself? That way, if there were a problem, the kids wouldn't be witnesses. That was him being a responsible father figure.

Avoid taking the kids into a situation where someone might kill me.

Very grown up.

He pulled his cell from his pocket. Maybe he should call Justin, warn him? But given the way things had been left between them, who knew what Justin would do? They'd promised to stay out of each other's lives, and so far Rob had kept this promise.

Also, turning up with the boys had to be a good move. Justin would be less likely to turn away children; no man would be that heartless.

They'd already seen enough today and had been quiet since the accident. Or at least quiet since that whole Uncle-Rob-Is-A-Hero nonsense.

I can't keep doing shutting them down by ignoring them. But it won't matter once they were settled at Crooked Tree. Then they would be someone else's problem.

He clenched his fists. How fucked was he that he saw his own nephews as a problem?

Pull yourself together, Brady, stick to the plan. They'll thank you for it when they're older.

Decision made, he helped the two of them out of the car, and they immediately moved away from him and held hands.

"Bunny!" Toby exclaimed, and Rob pulled it out from where it had gotten stuck, handing the distinctly damp toy to his nephew.

"Don't let the horses get it." He wished he could've pulled the teasing words back when, instead of smiling, Toby winced and hunched in on himself, holding Bunny protectively.

See? You're shit at this!

They crossed the bridge over the Blackfoot River and up to the restaurant. He didn't know where Justin was now. Would he still be with Sam? They'd seemed made for each other. Sam, a chef, all sass and independence, and Justin, so broken and alone. Everyone should have a Sam, and Rob hoped they'd made it from lust to love. Justin deserved some happiness. After all, he hadn't had a choice working for the Unit. At least not the same choices as Rob had been given.

The restaurant was closed. The inside was in darkness, and he checked his watch. Eleven p.m. Kind of early for everyone to be in bed, but then, this was middle-of-nowhere Montana, and people likely worked on a different clock up here. He tapped on the door, but no lights came on, so he knocked again. Nothing.

"Okay kids, wait here." He stared up at the window right next to the full tree. In a few quick, but shaky motions, he swung himself up onto the first branch, and cursing at the pain in his back, he climbed up the tree, using the trunk and the wall until he could lean in through the open window. The bedroom was empty. In fact, the whole place seemed deserted. He let himself back down, stared past the restaurant and up to the rest of the houses. There were lights on. At least some evidence that people lived at Crooked Tree. Then, when he'd decided that going on up the hill was his next course of action, he heard voices, and one, in particular, he knew immediately.

In the dim lighting, he recognized Justin, holding hands with Sam and stopping to kiss him every few feet. Neither man had spotted the three of them, which worried Rob. Evidently, Justin-the-former-assassin had lost his edge.

Has Justin finally chilled out and stopped being a killing machine? Is he actually a human? Has he found a way out?

"Hey, Justin," he announced his presence.

In the blink of an eye, Justin had Sam behind him, his knees bent, ready to take on whoever waited in the dark

That's more like it. That's the Justin I remember.

"It's me." Rob held up his hands. He didn't know if Justin was armed or not, but he wasn't taking any chances.

Justin said something to Sam, waved for him to stay,

then carried on down the path toward them. Apparently, Sam didn't take well to orders and followed him immediately.

"What the fuck are you doing here, Rob?" Justin asked, with no attempt at civility. Behind Rob, Toby sniffed, and again Justin crouched a little more at the noise.

"Watch the cursing, J. I'm visiting with my nephews, Come. Come out, guys. This is Bran, Toby." The two of them shuffled to stand next to him, and Rob saw the moment dangerous-with-intent-to-harm-Justin changed into innocent-as-a-kitten Justin.

"What the fu—what is this?" he asked, glancing from Rob to the kids.

Time for absolute honesty with Justin, just like with the kids. No pretending. Lay it all out there. Or at least most of it.

"Justin, I didn't know where else to go."

"What did you do, Rob?"

"I became responsible for my nephews, overnight."

For a long time, he and Justin stared at each other. He waited for Justin to say something, or at least indicate that he was okay with this visit from his old partner.

"You need to leave, now," Justin raised his voice and stepped forward, the kids moving back just as fast.

"You can't hurt him!" Bran shouted, and pushed Toby behind him.

Sam pushed past Justin, glaring at his boyfriend, and came to a stop in front of the boys, crouching down to talk to them. "No one will hurt you. I promise. My name is Sam, do you want to go inside and get some hot chocolate and cookies? Leave your uncle and Justin to talk?"

"They're shouting," Bran said.

Sam looked back at Justin. "They won't shout any more," he warned.

Bran and Toby glanced at each other, and neither seemed as if they wanted to leave Rob.

"It's okay," Rob murmured to them, but the boys didn't move. They weren't budging from his side. "You can go. Sam is a friend."

If anything, Bran gripped his jacket tighter.

"I'll be five minutes," he said and unpeeled Bran's fingers. "Don't be silly now. You need to be grown up, go with Sam, and take care of your brother."

Bran allowed him to move his hand and stepped away; any confusion left his expression and he pushed his shoulders back.

"Come on, Toby," he said, "*I'll* look after you."

Remorse flooded Rob. He shouldn't have said that either, not called Bran silly, or forced him to be the responsible one. Bran was too little to be carrying the weight of something like that. Bran had been asking Rob for help, and Rob had pushed Bran away, probably broken his heart or something. Which just proved he was not cut out for being a parent at all. He knew he'd fucked up but couldn't find the words to immediately apologize, not when he had Justin to talk to.

Fuck you, Suzi, for leaving and for making me something I never thought I'd be.

"Let's get you into the warm, kids." Sam unlocked the restaurant door. "I have all kinds of cookies." His unspoken message was that he was giving Justin and Rob time to talk. Only when the door was locked again, with the kids and Sam inside, did Justin move. He pushed Rob up against the wall, a hand on his throat.

"Why are you here?" His lips curled in a snarl, temper flashing hot in his words.

"I told you already—"

"If you're here to hurt us—"

"No, jeez, I'm not part of that anymore. I told you last time—"

"Shut up, Rob."

They stared at each other, and then with a huff, Justin released him, and Rob sagged a little at the loss of his hold.

"Summarize," Justin demanded.

Now *that* he could do. "Sister dead, kidney cancer, father passed away some years ago. She left two boys, and she had no way to contact me at any time. So yeah, I fucked up there. Then, God knows why, but even though I'd vanished from her life, she named me their guardian. I pulled three days surveillance, didn't like what I saw where they were, then worked up a plan on a favor from that New York job with Governor Chilton's son nine years ago. End result I have two children to get situated, so I need a bed for them, and obviously, for me."

Justin observed him as he spoke. "What the hell, Rob? Are you fucking with me?"

"I swear it's all true. We never lied to each other. Not once in all the time we worked together did we lie."

Of course, he would be lying soon. Not about the backstory, but when it came to future intentions? Now that was going to be a huge misdirection of truth.

Justin crossed his arms over his chest. "Are you hiding? Or escaping from something? Someone?"

"No."

"Swear to me that my family is safe." Justin moved closer. "Swear to me that you being here won't put them in danger."

Rob understood the deep paranoia and fear, as it was real to him as well.

"I swear. The kids need a family; I need a friend, and, Justin, you're about the only person I've ever called a friend."

Justin huffed a laugh then, a bitter laugh like chalk on a blackboard. "You must be desperate to say that shit."

Rob followed Justin into the restaurant, and all he could think was one thing.

I was telling the truth. You are my only friend.

And how fucked up was Rob to get to thirty-one and not have one single friend in the world other than a former assassin you'd once worked with?

Chapter Four

JUSTIN RELUCTANTLY GAVE THEM THE KEYS TO A CABIN THAT
he said was an old staff place, underlining the fact that he
expected Rob to stay one night and one night only. Rob
imagined that Sam had a lot to do with the decision and
thanked him for it.

But all Sam did was stare at him with accusation in
his eyes.

"Don't mess with Justin," he said when the kids weren't
listening.

"I promise," Rob said, and he meant it.

The kids chose a room, wanting to sleep together, and
after Rob had checked all security and locked them in,
Fentanyl was enough to let him rest.

But, when Rob woke to darkness, feeling like there was
someone in the room with him, he wasn't surprised to see
Justin on the window sill, a gun in his hand, backlit by the
moon and shadowed in the small bedside light next to Rob.

"One night, that's all," Justin repeated his earlier words.

"Justin—"

"One night."

"What if I need more time? What about the boys?"

"I don't want you here."

The words didn't hurt. How could they? Justin didn't need him hanging about reminding him of the remnants of a terrible life.

"I get that—"

"What the hell is going on with you?"

"Nothing. This is a vacation. Thinking time is all."

"You're lying."

"I'm not."

"You forget I know when you're lying."

"Are you going to use that gun?"

"Are you going to stop lying?"

He deliberately turned his back to Justin and pulled the sheet up over his shoulder. "Good night, J."

"You leave tomorrow," Justin replied. "You *and* the kids."

Rob knew when Justin had gone; he just had the sense of it.

How long could he keep his secrets to make this work? He didn't sleep again and gave up even trying a little after dawn. He sat for hours with coffee on his porch staring up at the mountains.

Nothing like a bullet killing me slowly to make me appreciate all the simple things I hadn't done before.

Like looking at mountains, or listening to rivers, or watching reruns of old TV shows from his childhood.

I'm getting sentimental. Sitting here feeling sorry for myself, wallowing in self pity, won't get things done.

He'd hardly slept at all, worried about the room, the cabin, and Justin's less than friendly welcome and predawn visit. It had taken him a long time to prioritize the issues in his head and come up with a workable solution.

Then he gave himself time to worry about the kids and the shape of their future.

And now it was ten a.m., and Rob had tried everything to get Bran and Toby to move from their bedroom. They hadn't come out this morning for food, so the day hadn't really started. And he needed to get it started, going up to see Justin and convincing him that letting him and the boys stay was a good thing.

Anyway, breakfast was nothing special, just some of the last few energy bars that Rob had picked up last night at the gas station and cartons of orange juice.

"Come on kids, up and at 'em."

"We're okay here," Bran said from his position on the bed, although Toby didn't seem as if he agreed, not until his brother spoke for him.

That wasn't healthy, right? Toby hadn't expressed a single thought that he hadn't passed by his brother first. They probably needed counseling or support from someone who wasn't an absentee uncle. He pushed a hand through his hair and then gripped it, unsure what to do next.

They ate the cereal bars for a really late breakfast, washed down with orange juice, and finally Rob reached the limit of being able to sit around watching the kids stare back at him with accusation in their eyes.

"We could go for a walk." He waited for Bran to argue. "Get out of the cabin, maybe go find some real food?"

Ignore the fact that Justin wants us gone today.

"No, thank you, Uncle Rob," Bran replied.

"I know," he ignored Bran. "We can go see the horses; I promised you horses." Every kid liked animals, right? "And fresh air, we need that, right?"

Bran considered what he said, then nodded. "We won't go near horses, but we should probably get some air."

Jeez, Bran sounded so grown up, older than his eight years. Then Bran helped Toby off the bed. Surely Toby didn't need his big brother to help, but Rob could see he was leaning on Bran and kept checking with him. Toby was a healthy five-year-old boy. Shouldn't he be bouncing from bed to bed? Or was he genuinely this needy at five? What had Toby seen in his life? Did he feel as if he had no place in the world? Or was it something else?

I have no fucking idea.

He breathed a huge sigh of relief when they moved, having spent the last hour thinking the two of them would stay in their room forever. Unless he got them out of the cabin, he'd never be able to start working on finding someone to take the kids. Or persuade Justin to let them stay by showing him what good kids they were.

Then he had another worry to consider. Should he supervise what they were wearing? Was that what he needed to do first? He guessed that is what responsible adults did, so he crossed to their bags and peered inside the first one. Bran moved so fast that he stumbled backward, Bran getting right in front of him.

"That's my bag," he said with force and determination.

"Sorry, I was just looking for uhmmm, clothes, and things."

Bran crossed his arms over his chest, and it reminded Rob of when Suzy had been that age, fiercely independent and utterly focused. He moved away and raised his hands in a gesture of innocence. He'd faced down terrorists, royalty, even the president, but one small boy, and he was on dangerous ground.

"I'll be in the uhm… out there."

He left them, picking up his phone, the key to the cabin, and retrieving his weapon. He didn't have anywhere to leave it, apart from the lockbox in the car, which was a shit place if the car was stolen at all. So, at the moment the gun was on top of his closet. Super-high up so that even he had to stretch to reach it. He hoped that Justin might have an internal lockbox or a safe for him to keep it in. Rob trusted Justin with his gun. Actually, Justin was the *only* one he'd ever trusted with anything that Rob thought valuable.

His gun. His life. The missions they'd run together.

Justin was solidly his to lean on. Or at least he had been until he found out he'd been lied to by the men who'd hired him, and that his life had been destroyed.

Any friendship they might have had was finished when Justin became the hunted one, and it was Rob's job to find him. How quickly their team had unraveled, turning up lies and errors, showing that he and Justin had sometimes been used to kill people for political or monetary gain without their knowledge. Hell, he'd been sent to kill Justin just to stop him talking, and how fucked-up was that?

With the gun tucked into the back of his jeans, he at least felt like he had a backup. Against what, he wasn't sure, but it felt familiar and gave him confidence, in a world where he didn't truly fit.

"What's that?" Bran asked as Rob pulled his thick T-shirt down to cover it. He couldn't have got more than a glimpse, certainly wouldn't have seen it was a gun.

"Nothing," he lied. "Are you ready to go?"

By the time they were out, it was nearer to lunch than breakfast, and on the spur of the moment, he decided that they needed to stay out of the cabin for as long as possible. That way he wouldn't have to deal with Bran's accusing expressions or Toby's tears. He considered getting them in the car and going for a drive, but no. Small space, just the three of them? Not happening. Anyway, the point of this visit was to get the kids to connect to everyone here so they wouldn't feel abandoned when he left. Driving off the ranch wouldn't serve any purpose.

Wide open spaces. A picnic maybe? That sounded like the kind of thing that would give them all space, get them used to the ranch, maybe hook up with some of the people who lived there. They could play somewhere, do things that kids did. Maybe run around some, and Rob could consider the plans he needed to make for them.

He could engineer things so that they accidentally met up with Justin and Sam. Which reminded him that he needed to start writing notes on his thoughts as he met the others here, and he should do it soon if he only planned on staying a week. He'd already decided Justin would make a good dad. The man was a mess of ethics and family love, and had a desperate need to do the right thing. Where Rob lacked compassion, Justin had too much. Except when it came to letting him, and the boys stay more than a night.

What could Justin do? Change the locks on the staff cabin? Put all their belongings in a pile next to the car? Would he even do that?

"Food. Actually, a picnic. Sounds good?" he asked the kids, watching Bran frown, and Toby glance up at his brother with a hopeful expression on his face, his big brown eyes full of excitement. Had Rob managed to do something right with his nephew for the first time?

"We love picnics," Bran finally offered somewhat reluctantly, and Toby nodded.

Rob crouched in front of them. "What kind of things do you like to eat?" He couldn't just go in and get loads of junk. He might not want to be their dad, but he wasn't messing with their nutrition either.

"Ham," Bran announced.

"What about you, Toby?"

His nephew stared at the ground, and Bran moved a little, drawing his attention. "He likes cheese and ham, and chips."

Toby refused to meet Rob's eyes, but he nodded vigorously. Someone needed to get through to the little boy, a mother figure or something. He recalled that one of Justin's friends was married to a woman who happened to be a mom. She'd have an idea of what to do with Toby. He added that to his mental list and took them into the small shop next to the restaurant, Branches. He didn't recognize the assistant in there, but his name badge said Edgar, which seemed like an old-fashioned name to give someone who had to be only eighteen or so.

"Morning," Edgar said with a grin. "What can I get you?"

Bran and Toby stayed by the door, but the fridge was right there with drinks, and there was a shelf of chip bags neatly arranged in rainbow order, so it wasn't difficult. He picked up chips and sodas, with a healthy amount of water, and exchanged small talk with Edgar.

"Do you have any sandwiches or rolls or something?"

"They do that kind of thing at Branches," Edgar said helpfully.

Branches. An excellent chance to find someone in there to start the delicate negotiation over who was going to take in Bran and Toby.

Hope pricked at Rob when he saw that Justin was in Branches, drinking coffee at the counter, talking to Sam, who Rob knew enough to smile at, after their late night arrival.

He went right up to the counter, taking the stool next to Justin. Bran and Toby were on his heels, waiting patiently.

"Hey."

Justin side-eyed him, and half nodded instead of actually engaging in conversation. A simple "Hi" might have been nice, but they'd never done the polite shit, spending any time together working up plans or figuring out kill angles.

"You're still here," he said.

"And we're staying."

"One day is all I said you could—"

"Can I get some filled rolls or something?" Rob ignored Jason and spoke directly to Sam. "Two with ham, one with ham and cheese."

Sam took the order, and with a quick glance at Justin, he went back into the kitchen, keeping the door open so he could see them.

What had Justin told Sam about him?

He turned to talk to Justin.

"Leave me alone," Justin snapped before he could say anything else.

Sam arrived back, and hell, that was the fastest sandwich making he'd ever experienced. He placed those and a see-through container on the counter.

"There's some pasta in there as well. Help yourself to forks from the takeout area." It seemed Sam was now waiting for him to leave. Justin shifted on his stool as if he was making a move as well, and Rob didn't have time to wait any longer. He had to get things started now while he still could.

"Justin, you've met Bran and Toby," he blurted and leaned down to shuffle them closer to Justin. Bran balked a little, then allowed himself to be moved, along with his brother.

Justin looked down at them, a half smile on his face. The smile was a new one to Rob. He couldn't remember a time when he'd ever seen Justin genuinely smile, even if this particular half grimace was a little forced to start.

"Hi," he said.

"They wanted to talk to you," Rob said, and had three

pairs of eyes turn to him. Bran was confused, Sam raised an eyebrow, and Justin frowned.

"Horses," Rob said quickly. "The kids would like to learn to ride."

"We never said that." Bran was loud.

"This isn't a fucking vacation with extras," Justin muttered under his breath at the same time.

"It will be fun," Rob said to Bran and then more directly to Justin, "I can pay."

Justin shook his head, then stood and leaned close. "Fuck's sake, Rob. Why did you even come here? One night and you should be gone."

"I'll book a proper cabin; I'm not looking for charity. Hell J, I have money—"

"We don't *need* your money." Justin was loud, and a couple of chairs scraped behind them, likely other patrons wanting to take a look at whatever was going down. Toby let out a squeak, and Bran gripped his hand and backed away.

Sam placed a hand on Justin's. "Dial it down."

Rob waited for Justin to snap back and yank his hand away from Sam's touch, but he didn't. Instead, he turned it over and laced their fingers. He never thought he'd see the day where Justin could be calmed by another person's touch.

"My money is as good as the next person's," Rob insisted and waited for Justin to tear him a new one.

All he did was sigh heavily. "Hurry up and leave," he said. Then leaning over to kiss Sam gently, he walked out of Branches, stopping briefly to say something to Bran who was now just outside the door.

"Sorry," Rob apologized to Sam, again, but a customer paying their check interrupted any chance of small talk, and Rob needed to go out to Bran and Toby anyway. Justin was long gone.

"What did he say to you?" Rob asked Bran.

"He asked how long we're staying. I told him we didn't know."

"Okay."

Bran looked at Rob, and there was an adult expression in his eyes, full of something that seemed a lot like an accusation. "Do you know?"

They'd moved away from Branches, and he'd missed something. "Know what?"

"How long we're staying."

"A long time," was all Rob could offer because if he had his way, Bran and Toby were staying here forever.

They headed past the horses and into the trees beyond the owners' accommodation. He knew they were on the wrong side of the river. This was private, and the signs said so, but something Justin had once said about the lake up on the mountainside had him thinking this was an excellent direction to take. Anyway, it would take him past the owners' houses, and he could maybe meet some of them and at least start a conversation.

After all, the one with Sam and Justin didn't go so well.

He glanced back at Bran and Toby following him like a duckling after a momma duck, holding hands, Bran all serious and staring ahead, Toby's eyes still wide, checking everything out, cataloging every new experience. Compassion poked at him. What kind of life had they had for the past year? And what about before? Had Suzi been a good mom? His sister had always been the flighty one, living for the moment, but some man had managed to get her settled into at least having kids, he guessed. Both their birth certificates gave the name of Richard Hastings as the father, but he was long gone, dead at twenty-eight from sepsis after surgery on his appendix. What must it have been like to lose their dad, even if Bran had only been four at the time and Toby a babe in arms? And then their mom?

And now Bran and Toby didn't have a dad or a mom, and all they did have was one fucked-up uncle who was losing his shit over what to do with them.

Someone else who will leave them.

Eyes forward, he carried on past the last house, coming to a gently flowing creek that ultimately would lead to the river below. They were maybe forty feet above the river here, and the water was in a broad basin that was deep in the middle and calm. The day was hot, the water cold, and the itch to get in there was strong.

"Afternoon folks, can I help you?" a voice came from his left, and Rob schooled his features into complete innocence as he turned.

"Hi," he said and felt Bran bump into him. Toby moved closer.

"I think you took a wrong turn," the man said and moved out of the sunlight, closer to them. He was tall and gorgeous, in worn jeans and a plaid shirt, a cowboy hat on his head. "No problem, I can help out. Were you looking for the horses?" He gestured down the hill to the stables. They'd gotten to that point, but neither Bran or Toby had seemed interested on getting close to the horses, hence they'd moved on.

"I'm a friend of Justin's," he said calmly focusing on the reaction from the big cowboy. "Rob. And these are my nephews, Bran and Toby."

"Hi. Sam said Justin had friends staying. Nice to meet you. I'm Nate Todd," the cowboy said and extended a hand for Rob to shake. They took the measure of each other briefly, and then Nate smiled. "You walking up to the lake?"

Nate Todd. The oldest of the three Todd brothers. It was the middle brother, Gabe, who Rob wanted to meet, the married one with kids. That was another family Bran and Toby would be better off with. Still, he might have to go through Nate to get to Gabe, and he still had Sam and Justin on his list as priority parents.

"Justin always said it was a cool place for kids."

There, lie a little and turn the conversation back to Bran and Toby. Just as he hoped, Nate crouched down to their level, removing his Stetson and offering his hand to Bran who shook it, and then to Toby who didn't let go of Bran but gave his other hand.

"You're going to love the lake," he said. "You like horses?"

Bran wrinkled his nose and then shrugged. "They're kinda scary."

Nate nodded with a serious expression on his face. "Some of them are, but we have a couple of smaller ones that love children. You should come to visit. Ask for Nate."

"Yes, sir," Bran answered and then gave Nate a cautious smile. Which was more than Rob had ever received. Nate had a way with children, and Rob knew he was in a relationship with someone called Jay. They'd make another set of potential parents, he was sure of it.

"We could do that now," he said, ignoring the fact he'd promised a picnic and a visit to the lake.

Nate shook his head. "Sorry, guys, I'm booked out now, but I'll be there after dinner tonight if you want to come up."

He stood, put his hat back on, winked, and then left, walking down the hill and whistling tunelessly.

His plan to interact with Nate was thwarted. They carried on up the hill, but this time he held back a little, so he was walking at Bran and Toby's slower pace while they strolled ahead holding hands. Both were in jeans that looked clean, but Toby's were a little short in the leg, and Rob resolved to buy some more, along with whatever else they'd need that fit them. He added this to his mental list. Just after adding Nate's name as possible dad material.

When the path opened up to the glacial lake, he could see precisely why Justin had talked about it when they'd had downtime. He'd always sounded so wistful about Crooked Tree, and the lake and the horses. He'd often said his soul would only be entirely happy if he could go home.

Not that Justin had ever planned to go home and so went about life with dedication to his country and a hole in his heart. Rob had never entirely understood Justin; they were so different. But he had understood that beauty was something that other people could carry inside themselves. The lake was stunning, the soaring mountains reflected in the water, rock formations tumbling haphazardly on one side. Isolation and peace.

Only they weren't at the lake alone. A man standing with his back to them stared at the water. He must have heard them arrive, and turned to face them, and Rob would have recognized him anywhere.

The EMT from the crash scene.

Army.

The EMT recognized Rob right back, but he didn't smile in welcome.

"What are you doing here, Navy?" he asked.

This was Rob's first proper look at the competent, hard man who was masquerading as an EMT in this backwater county. He was built, broad, apparently worked out, and his bright blue eyes were gorgeous.

"Army," Rob said back, pushing down the shot of lust he'd felt at first seeing the man who'd tried to order him out of the car. Stupid because even with his reasonably accurate gaydar, two alphas did not end up fucking. Nope. Shame because Army was one hot dude in board shorts and a bright pink T-shirt with a unicorn farting rainbows front and center. That pretty much confirmed the sexual spectrum status of him right there.

It might be a good idea to exchange proper names instead of defining each other by their respective theaters of war.

"Rob," he introduced himself, and Army turned back to stare over the lake.

"I would shake your hand," Army said, "but I am not moving from this spot until the kids are back on dry land."

For a second Rob got confused and thought the man was talking about Bran and Toby, and then he glanced past him to the two small figures near the rocks at the center of the lake. They were swimming vigorously, and a sharp stab of envy speared him. He hadn't chosen to be a SEAL lightly; he'd love swimming as a child, spent hours in the sea near his home on the Chesapeake.

Being in the water was good. It was healthy and fun, and maybe next time he came up here with Bran and Toby, they could bring things. He was good at swimming, and it would tire them out. Perhaps he could get Justin in the water with them or Nate or anyone.

The silence was weird. He could ignore the man watching the children, or he could try and channel a real-life 'normal' persona again. Decision made, he walked the five steps between them and extended his hand, which the EMT took.

"I'm Aaron by the way," tall, blond, and sexy said.

Aaron's hand was warm, his grip firm. They held brief eye contact, sizing each other up. But it wasn't long enough, and he stared at the children heading back from the rocks to shore, a good thirty feet. Both of them strong swimmers. Rob guessed if they'd grown up there, then it was like where he had spent his childhood, water on the doorstep, swimming from an early age.

"I thought this place was private," Rob said.

"I know the family," Aaron explained. "Special dispensation. You?"

"Justin's friend," he said and couldn't quite meet Aaron's eyes, because *'friend'* was a step too far for Justin, given his reactions thus far to Rob being there.

"Uncle Rob?" Bran asked and tugged on his shirt. Jeez. Jeez, he'd forgotten all about them after one look into Aaron's thoughtful sapphire gaze.

Rob crouched by him to hear better. "Yes?"

Bran stared up at Aaron pointedly and then back at Rob. Great. He was being shown social skills from his eight-year-old nephew. He needed to up his game to care for his new charges and find them their forever home. That started with not lusting over gorgeous men who had a specific way about them. That would have to change, from today. Of course, going to his knee was the wrong thing to do, his back protesting. Although no one would know, if they were watching him that he was in any pain at all. He was excellent at hiding his shit.

"These are my nephews Bran and Toby."

Aaron copied him, eyes still half on the water, crouching and holding out his hand. "Hi guys, you like swimming?"

That was a stupid question; all kids loved swimming. Rob remembered the hours he would spend in the local lake, then the pool, feeling more at home in the water, splashing around with friends, and holding his breath longer than any of them.

"Toby can't swim," Bran said. "I can, but Toby is scared."

If Aaron was surprised by that, he didn't give anything away, but Rob wasn't just surprised; he was shocked. Hadn't his sister thought to teach Toby? Every kid needed to learn how to swim for god's sake.

"But you like the water, right, Toby?" Rob gestured at the beautiful lake under the warm sun. Who couldn't love a place like this? He'd seen it on his last fact-finding mission here before approaching Justin that previous time, and right now part of him had longed to walk into the water and never come out.

Bran answered for him. "He doesn't know."

Toby dropped his gaze and mumbled something, and Aaron leaned in.

"What was that, Toby?" he asked gently.

"I like baths," Toby said.

"And Momma tried to take Toby to lessons, but her car broke, and then she was ill, and we never went back," Bran explained.

Rob was quietly horrified at the casual way they mentioned their mom being ill, and also that Toby had never learned to swim.

"We need to get you some swimsuits, and I can show Toby how to swim." Swimming was like learning to ride a bike, a rite of passage for every kid. That was one thing he could do before he left. The kids wouldn't form any attachment to him just because he taught them to swim.

Bran glanced at the water dubiously, then back at his uncle. Rob felt as if he was under a microscope, being judged and found wanting. This was a test. Did Bran trust him enough to think he could take care of them?

"Maybe. But you gotta hold onto Toby the whole time."

There it was again, that inbuilt fathering complex that the kid shouldn't have at his age.

"I will."

He wanted to offer Bran his finger, do some kind of pinkie swear. That's what kids did, right?

He'd laugh you out of Montana.

They were interrupted by the arrival of the children who'd been swimming, clambering up natural stone steps that led from the water to the small, pebbled shore. Aaron had towels and efficiently wrapped the two of them up, with laughter and smiles. Then they bundled over to Rob, Bran and Toby like excited puppies, with Aaron not far behind.

Within five seconds, Milly and Jake, as they introduced themselves, had asked the other two to play. They had a den, apparently, and a picnic.

Bran glanced up at him as if he was asking permission, but there was also fear in his eyes. Wait. Was he seeking reassurance? From him?

"What if there are snakes?" he asked, oh so very seriously. "Toby won't like snakes."

"You want me to check it out?"

Bran nodded, and it seemed as if it was on Rob to make sure the den was safe. He should've felt wrong for that. He wasn't here in Bran's life to be someone he could rely on, but something in his expression reminded him so much of Suzy.

Rob, I'm scared of the water. Help me.

Rob shook his head to clear the memories of them on the shoreline, him trying to teach his sister to swim. That first time had been so good, holding her up as he showed her how easy it was to move through the water. She'd looked at him with adoration on that day, the kind of hero worship that had made him feel like the strongest kid on the block.

Seemed like he'd gotten used to being the one in charge, the hero for saving the day, way too early in life.

"The den is just there." Aaron interrupted his memories, and pointed to a rock with some branches laid on it. The whole construction appeared sturdy enough, and Rob walked over with all four kids in tow. He speedily checked the stability and whether any wild critters had taken hold. Inside was a mini palace, with blankets, a big icebox container, and cushions. And certainly no snakes of any sort. Not even under the pillows and covers.

"We do this every Sunday," Aaron explained. "We cart everything up here, and they make a den."

"It's safe," Rob confirmed to Bran and Toby and watched carefully as the four children went inside. His nephews sat quietly while the other two began raiding the icebox, but they at least took the offered snacks.

"Drink?" Aaron reached into the den and pulled out two bottles of water, offering one to Rob, which he took gratefully. It was warm, and even though it was late afternoon, it was still the kind of weather that everyone needed to keep hydrated, and he'd already drunk the water he'd bought himself.

"Thanks," Rob took a long drink, wiping his mouth with the back of his hand, and caught Aaron staring at him. There was no doubt there was something in his expression that spoke of hunger. He made sure to let his gaze linger, to confirm that, yep, he was interested.

Who wouldn't be interested in Aaron, the paramedic? He was precisely the kind of guy that Rob found attractive. It was just a pity they weren't in some random club. Then they could fuck and get it over with. Of course, they'd need to decide who was in charge, and of course, that would be Rob because no one told him what to do. Aaron quirked a smile and unscrewed the cap to his water. A few drops fell onto his hand as he drank.

Is it just me or is watching a guy drink and finding it sexy a serious lust marker?

He coughed to clear his throat and wished he could shove his hands down his pants to rearrange his thickening cock. Thank god his jeans were worn and a little loose on him.

"So what do you do when your two are playing in there?" He needed to get the conversation back on track and away from thoughts of sex.

Aaron gestured with the Kindle in his left hand. "Sit and read mostly."

Rob ran out of questions and then recalled the one he should be asking. "The guy in the accident, is he okay?"

Aaron smiled then, and it was a gorgeous, soft, sexy smile. He had cute dimples, and his sapphire eyes shone.

"He's doing well. My brother said he'd got all the information he needs, said he asked you questions but wants a written statement, yeah? He thinks it was a brake issue on the semi as it was coming off the ridge."

It hit Rob then why there was something familiar about Aaron. Give him dark hair, make him taller, and it was evident that Aaron was related to the sheriff who'd asked him questions at the wreck.

"The sheriff, right?"

"My little brother, and yeah, I know he's like five inches taller than me and built big, but yeah, baby brother."

They fell into silence, Aaron clambering up to sit cross-legged on a rock and Rob deciding that it was safe to stare at the water.

"You were a fucking idiot; you know that," Aaron said.

Rob turned to face him. "It needed two of us idiots to get it done."

Aaron shrugged. "I get paid to deal with that."

"You know damn well you don't get paid enough to put yourself in harm's way."

Aaron laughed at that, resting his hands on his knees. "It's not always car crashes, you know. Sometimes it's ferrying old man Ester from home to clinic and back. My other brother is the one who puts himself in harm's way. Jason, the firefighter. You met him on the scene."

"So. Paramedic, firefighter, cop? You're one of three adrenaline junkie brothers?"

"One of five, although second in the lineup is Eddie. He's not an adrenaline junkie by any stretch of the imagination. Then there is big brother, Saul; he runs Carters. You should check it out." Aaron tipped his face up to the sun's rays as it dropped behind the clouds. The air was still warm, but the breeze off the lake was a reminder that the temperature would likely drop later, here in the shadow of the mountain.

"Check what out?"

"Carters bar. It's outside of town, not far, got some rooms out the back, a clean place to eat, drink, and fuck. Could be the best place to meet other guys to scratch that itch you got going on there."

Rob stiffened and crossed his arms over his chest. "I don't even know you, and you don't get to tell me where I go to fuck someone."

Or get fucked.

They were far enough away from the kids to talk freely, but even so, his sex life was not up for discussion. He knew what he wanted. Some nameless hookups that filled what was left of his time here while he still could, but it wouldn't be on his doorstep.

"Just trying to help," Aaron gave one of those I-don't-care-what-you-do shrugs.

"Is that where you go then?" Rob wanted to get to Aaron as much as Aaron was trying to mess with him.

"Me?" Aaron was comically horrified. "I grew up at Carters. I'm not going to hookup in the family home."

"You grew up in a brothel?"

Aaron's expression became guarded, and he sat forward, uncrossing his legs and letting them dangle over the edge of the boulder. He was coiled and ready to leap. Rob didn't have to be a former SEAL to recognize the thinly veiled aggression that sat beneath the surface of Aaron's otherwise benign expression.

"My brother gave us a home, and he offers anyone a safe place to meet. Alongside being a family pub, a place to dance, to socialize, it's a hub for the town and not a brothel."

"Whatever you say, Army. If it quacks like a duck…"

Aaron jumped down from the rock, and Rob had a moment to envy that the man's knees were still up to that kind of maneuver before he was right up in Rob's face.

They faced off for a few moments, and Rob could see the darker irises of blue around Aaron's eyes and the way his blond hair was loose, not gelled back as it had been at the scene of the accident. It fell onto his forehead and gave him a don't-care kind of appearance.

"What a damn shame," Aaron murmured, so close that Rob felt the breath of his words across his face. "That you're so hot" he paused, then deliberately leaned even closer, pressing his thumb to Rob's lips "but also such an asshole."

He stepped back then, and thank god he did because Rob was swaying toward him, imagining Aaron on his knees, and losing the tight control he had on his libido at the simple touch of him. He could imagine himself on his knees, sucking Aaron off, Aaron's thumb opening his mouth wider.

Jesus. What is wrong with me?

Aaron collected his two, the makings of the den. All four children complained they wanted to stay, even Bran and Toby.

"You know I promised your dad to get you back." Aaron smiled and hugged, and Rob didn't move the entire time.

"Later," Aaron said, and then with a sketchy wave, they walked back down the hill.

Which left him, Bran, and Toby standing there, all three of them looking a little lost.

"We should get back too," he said with a smile, but Bran had gone back to wary and quiet, and Toby was sucking on one ear of his bunny. He held up the bag of sandwiches he was still clutching. "Or do you want to eat here?"

Bran reached for Toby's hand and shook his head. "Let's go back before it's dark."

Rob didn't explain that it was a long time until dark. He just followed them down the hill and thought about Aaron and the children, and just what the hell he was doing with what was left of his life.

Nothing much of any importance, it seemed.

By the time they reached the bridge, he felt renewed determination to get his nephews their forever home and for him to get the hell out of Dodge.

That was going to have to wait though because Sheriff Carter was standing by his car, evidently waiting for him.

"Sir," the sheriff said and stepped closer.

That didn't sound like a good start; not so much the words but the tone which held accusation.

"Sheriff," he replied, then touched Bran's shoulder. "You go ahead, boys. Wait for me at the door." Then he looked back, ready to face down whatever was causing issues.

"Permits check out," Sheriff Carter began. "I just have something I need to clear up."

"Go on."

He paused for a moment, then sighed. "You're a friend of Justin's," he said.

"Is that a statement or a question?"

"I'm aware of the *career* that took Justin from his family for so long. I assume that he knows you from that time." He held up a hand to stop Rob talking. "I get that it's classified, but there are families here on the ranch," the sheriff began patiently. "Do I have to worry?"

Then he merely stared at Rob.

"No." That was all Rob could give, and it was about the only real truth he had in his arsenal right now.

"Okay then," Ryan seemed to take his words at face value. "I have a report for you to check." He handed over the board, a pen, and the statement, which Rob read from beginning to end, then signed.

The sheriff thanked him, and Rob threw out something about the kids not being able to get in, and it would be dark soon.

God knows why he added that last part because the sheriff cast a look at the blue sky and frowned.

So Rob left and hurried after the kids before the sheriff asked him what the hell he was talking about.

It was safer that way.

Chapter Five

AARON KNEW HE SHOULD'VE BEEN CONCENTRATING ON THE meeting, but too often since yesterday, he'd spent a hell of a lot of time thinking about Rob. Stupid really because the man was exactly what Aaron should be avoiding. He had secrets behind his steady green gaze. Former Navy, and from the way he held himself—confidence, arrogance, the surety that he could handle anything thrown at him, he had to be Special Forces. Or at least he had been.

But, there was something else in that expression of his that battled against the confidence. Wariness? Exhaustion? And the way he'd winced when he crouched? That man was in pain. Aaron had seen soldiers in pain before, hiding what they were feeling, pushing through, determined to finish an op or not let their team down.

Idiots with their heroics and disregard for their own lives.

Of course, there was also the line, " I'm a friend of Justin's." What kind of friend? Aaron had been the one to patch up Justin, digging a bullet out of him, off the record. He'd heard enough to know that Justin had been involved in some shady shit, but no one had offered anything more in the way of information, not even his brother, Ryan, who had known more about what happened to Justin than he'd let on.

Shady shit was such a good description for whatever Rob had going on in his head, but he also had the children with him. Bran and Toby, quiet kids, whose backstory was likely just as complicated.

How did one enigmatic man with palpable pain issues and an expression full of secrets end up vacationing with his nephews? Where were the parents, and why wasn't there an obvious connection between the three of them? The kids acted as if Rob was a stranger and not their uncle.

"Earth to Aaron," someone catcalled, and he snapped back to the meeting, which had clearly started while he'd been lost in his thoughts.

"Sorry," he apologized, but no one called him on his inattention.

Aaron sat back in the chair, part of the circle of veterans who were just about to start a session dealing with personal health. He'd seen his share of things overseas, and talking things out meant he could lessen the experiences and images that were trapped inside him. He tried to sit in on as many meetings at Hepburn House as he could, particularly when there was a new, recently arrived *guest* staying there.

This newbie was Lieutenant Lacey McAdams, coming up on the end of her third week and, up to now, quiet in all the sessions. That wasn't unusual for a newcomer to Hepburn House. When it started as a single place in the mountains of Tennessee, run by a former soldier, it had been a safe place for veterans to talk, to heal, to be with each other. To date, there were ten such places, and this was Aaron's home away from home.

Lacey had stuck to the usual path of least resistance since

arriving, where it was easier to listen than to lay herself bare. Today though, a switch had been flipped, and she was opening up about her time overseas, and in particular, finding her best friend trying to kill herself. How they had gotten to that was anyone's guess, but Aaron had seen the subtle way she'd crafted the conversation because it seemed to him that the near-death of her friend was the core of her issues and tied into her own PTSD.

None of the conversations were led. No one person sat down and said, "okay let's talk about PTSD." It just happened. An organic process that was incredibly painful.

"Of course, being a woman, her trying to commit suicide was put down as being a woman or 'hormones,' but when I found Lyn in the bathrooms hacking at her wrists, I knew that this wasn't some kind of monthly shit. This was real honest despair. She and I, women, we have all the same symptoms of PTSD as men, the hyper-arousal, re-experiencing, avoidance, and numbing. It's no different because we don't have dicks." She laughed then, but it was hollow, and no one laughed with her; this was too serious. "PTSD related to on-the-job incidents isn't just something that needs to viewed from the male perspective."

One of the others, Sean, a young man barely in his twenties, leaned forward and nodded.

"I get that, I do," he began, and Aaron could hear the *but*. He felt the tension ramp up in the room. What god-awful gender-specific crap was Sean going to spout now? "I guess the funding and research goes to the majority, and that is shit. All the researchers would need to do is include more women in the initial trials and counseling, and then it would benefit everyone."

The tension immediately subsided. Sean, former Marine, eyesight destroyed in one eye, hearing loss, and lower left arm amputation, apparently wasn't an asshole who needed to be ignored.

Now, it was Lacey's turn. "Men are more likely to feel angry, prone to abusing alcohol or drugs to deal."

Sean patted his prosthetic arm and nodded. "Drugs are good," he said and smiled wryly.

Everyone laughed with him, including Aaron. He'd had his share of seeing people pop pills to get through the day and considered himself lucky that he'd managed to avoid them. It wasn't for the lack of trying, but every time he'd tried to numb the pain of everything he'd seen and done, Elijah's ghost had pulled him back from the edge. He didn't know whether to be resentful or pleased that he couldn't shake the memories of the man he'd briefly loved and lost in the war.

Mary, the leader for this session, more like a guidance counselor than the highly qualified shrink she was, moved to summarize, helping to keep the conversation going.

"Women tend to have trouble feeling emotions and are prone to developing anxiety or depression, not drug dependency as much as men."

Lacey snorted a laugh. "See, we even miss out on the drugs part."

She and Sean exchanged glances and smiles, and Aaron sensed there could be a friendship in the making. Gallows humor about what they'd all seen and done.

They split for coffee. Aaron checked his watch, given it was Sunday morning, and he'd agreed to get himself over to Carters Bar for food with his brothers and their growing families. If he left now, he'd be early. That way he could help Saul, get a million brownie points, and not have to wash up after. Also, it gave him time to play with the kids, and that was the highlight of Sunday dinner. When he wasn't on shift, Sundays involved a session at the center, dinner with his brothers, and then off to Crooked Tree with his niece and nephew for their riding lessons. The perfect day then ended with a beer and chilling on his back porch with the view of the mountains.

He considered his last visit to Crooked Tree had ended in him getting up in the face of that sexy enigma, Rob. Still, that didn't mean he wasn't interested in talking to the man again. Maybe exchange a few war stories or something.

Yeah, that is such a shit idea.

"This coffee is appallingly bad," Lacey said at his elbow, coffee and donut in hand.

"Donuts help." He picked up the coffee he'd just poured and sipped the bitter brew. He wanted one of the ring donuts, but dinner at big brother's place was only two hours away. How could he win at eating the most of all the Carter brothers when space in his belly had been taken up by cake?

"Who's the new guy?" She inclined her head to mean Sean, or at least that's who Aaron thought she meant.

"Sean?"

"Hmmm, he's young, isn't he?"

Aaron couldn't pass on information like age or tours or injuries. This wasn't that kind of place, and Lacey was another of the guests here.

"You're not exactly old yourself."

She sighed and took a sip of coffee, grimacing and biting into her donut quickly. Only when she'd swallowed and licked the powdered sugar from the corner of her mouth did she quirk a smile.

"I'm at that point that we all hate, in my thirties and feeling so much older."

He nodded but felt the soft press of his approaching forty-third birthday keenly. Not that he didn't have something to show for his life. He'd saved lives in the war, and he'd worked at this house with veterans. He'd stayed as a paramedic in a town that couldn't afford all the extras he would have gotten in the city. He'd loved and lost, had his heart broken, and known the tragedy of holding a lover who'd died in his arms. He'd seen and achieved all kinds of things, and he was at peace with his age.

Most of the time.

Lust wasn't something he'd felt in a long while, but Rob with his green eyes, intense focus, and his secrets had stirred something in Aaron at the accident site. Not to mention their meeting at the lake with all that testosterone and sarcasm. Maybe it was time for him to find someone to be with, even just for one night, before his libido disappeared from lack of use.

But first, Sunday dinner with his family, the highlight of his week when he wasn't on shift. He headed straight for Carters, pleased to see Eddie's car in the parking lot. That meant his niece and nephew were there, and as soon as he walked in the kitchen, seeing Saul and Eddie talking loudly about the best way to cook carrots, he turned on his heel and went to find Milly and Jake. The kids were all kinds of awesome, and he loved spending time with them, so uncomplicated and innocent, and precisely what he needed. They'd built a convoluted tent system in the hallway off the kitchen, the same as they did every weekend, and he was used to crawling inside, but not before he had three attempts at this week's password.

"Sausages," he said.

"That's always your first try, Uncle Aaron," Milly fake-reprimanded and poked her head out of the entrance, her dark hair in two braids, her face split in a wide smile. "It's boring, and it's always wrong."

He considered himself told off. "Okay, how about kittens

then," he said and sat cross-legged in front of her on the carpet.

"He better not say tomato as usual," Jake's voice came from behind her.

"Shhh," Milly whispered loudly.

"Hmmm, my third guess is tomato?"

"Told ya he'd say it," Jake said with an exaggerated sigh. "He never remembers anything."

Given they changed the password each week, Aaron doubted his brain could recall a load of passwords, but he didn't say that, instead making them laugh by suggesting the same three things each week.

Milly held back the curtain of material that formed the door. "I guess you can come in if you like."

He crawled in, turning as he did so and finding the space he took whenever he was allowed inside.

"Hey guys," he said and accepted the hugs he was given.

"Uncle Aaron, my car is broke." Jake thrust the battered model Ferrari at him.

Aaron turned the tiny thing over in his hand. "What's wrong with it?" He wound the small key in the side that would give the car the oomph to move along the floor. He found out what was wrong with it when the key spun in the hole, and there was no sound of the band inside being wound up.

"It won't go," Jake said and frowned. He was one of those cute kids who melted everyone's hearts with the combination of his bright blue eyes and his pout. "But Dad said you can fix it."

Thanks, Eddie. Throw me to the wolves, why don't you.

"I'll take it with me and get it fixed up good as new, okay?"

That earned him another hug, and then he played for a

while, being typecast as a medic having to supply emergency care to Jake's teddy, which had a broken leg after falling off a horse at Crooked Tree. Or that was the story Jake was going with. Milly leaned against him reading out loud, and he could've quite happily stayed in the tent all day.

He always thought that one day he'd have kids of his own, but that hadn't happened. Still, he could be a damn good Uncle.

"I'm gonna canter today," Milly informed him. "Luke said I could."

Milly had a small crush on Luke Todd, back home from college on the weekends and spending his free time with the horses. He was the youngest of the Todd siblings and was good at teaching the kids how to ride.

"That's awesome."

"An' I'm gonna jump up and down on my saddle," Jake informed with a gap-toothed grin that spoke of mischief.

"No jumping in the saddle," Aaron murmured, making a mental note to mention that nugget of information to Luke. Jake had this way of pushing boundaries, but Aaron had caught this before it happened.

Only family was here, and he loved catching up with everything. When he and the kids crawled out of the tent just before two, the scent of steaks had filled the kitchen, and the large table was piled high with carrots, peas, potatoes, steaks, and the requisite steaming jug of Saul's special gravy. There were biscuits so fluffy that Aaron could swear they would float away, and he was desperate to dig in. Everything was being kept warm over little candle burners, and the only people at the table were Eddie, Jenny, and Saul.

"Where is everyone?" Aaron asked.

"The rest'll be through in a minute." Saul gestured for

him to sit. "Catching up with Jordan and Micah. We can wait."

"Fuck that," Aaron muttered under his breath so the kids wouldn't hear. Jordan was a Hollywood actor who'd fallen for the youngest of the Carter siblings, Sheriff Ryan. Everyone always had so many questions for him, but that shit wasn't as important as eating steak and potatoes. He left the table and then pushed open the door to the external bar, run by what Saul called his Sunday staff. He put two fingers in his mouth and whistled loudly to get the attention of the group of people standing at one end of the wooden counter. His brothers Jason and Ryan, plus boyfriend, boyfriend's twin, and twin's girlfriend.

"Dinner now, or it's gone," he announced and closed the door. First, at the table, give or take a brother or two, meant he got first pick on it all. When everyone finally sat down it was noisy and lively, and everybody was up in each other's business, and that was pretty much his idea of heaven.

"Aaron, how did that man do, the one from the accident?" Jason asked as he passed over the big bowl of potatoes.

Ryan took the question, given Aaron had a mouth full of potato and steak. "The driver? Last I heard he'll be out on Monday. We got to him in time."

And out alive, thanks to the help of one stubborn idiot Navy guy with green eyes.

Aaron helped himself to more potato and then assisted little Jake, who couldn't hold the bowl and scoop at the same time.

"Do we know who the other guy in the car was?" Jason asked. "The one who stayed with you and helped?"

"His name is Rob," Aaron said. "I don't know much else, but he's up at Crooked Tree. Former forces I think, and stupid stubborn."

He looked to Ryan for confirmation. As sheriff, he would surely have taken names and witnesses. After all, the accident had happened right in front of the man's SUV, so he must have had eyes on everything that happened.

Also, Aaron wanted to know the guy's reason for being at Crooked Tree because there was something else in that icy expression and arrogance, a pain that Aaron felt keenly.

"Yeah, Rob Brady, was traveling with his nephews in the back. He's not from around here but said he was staying up at Crooked Tree, although he was shady about how long. Said he's a friend of Justin. Seemed okay when I visited though, answered what I needed, and his credentials check out."

Interest poked at Aaron. There was something about the man that had him intrigued. He'd recognized another soldier, *sailor*, he corrected himself, a man who'd seen action. This Rob had been level-headed, known enough medicine to be helpful, calm in the face of the blood. He'd had the glacial calculation of someone who'd seen a lot and knew how to handle disaster. He was also all kinds of sexy. And annoying. And way too much of a top to ever make it good with Aaron.

Right?

"Earth to Aaron." Saul waved his fork in front of Aaron's face.

Aaron blinked back to whatever Saul had been saying, that he'd missed. "Sorry?"

"You spaced out," he observed, leaning closer. "Everything okay?"

"Oh, yeah, just some Hepburn House stuff on my mind."

"Like what?"

How did he get out of this one, when he'd been actually thinking about green eyes, a trimmed, neat beard, and dark hair that was thick and unruly. "Nothing to worry about," he said and gave Saul a look that said he couldn't talk.

Luckily, Saul didn't push, and it was over.

He collected the kids after they'd finished, ready to do uncle duty and take them to Crooked Tree Ranch, but he wasn't away fast enough. Eddie caught him as he was so very nearly away.

"Can I ask you something?" Eddie planted himself between Aaron and the door.

"Yeah. Kids, go wait in the truck." He pointed his key fob at his old Ford and pressed the button to release the locks. This was bound to be another question about Jenny's pregnancy, and he was happy to answer most of the questions, at least the ones with a medical slant.

Eddie leaned in as soon as the kids were safely in the truck, and lowered his voice. "Is it okay that a woman needs more sex when they're pregnant, do they get more... y'know... I mean Jenny wants it all the time, but will it hurt the baby if I... y'know."

Aaron's mouth fell open. Was Eddie seriously telling him about the state of his sex life? "You did not just ask me that, asshole," he said and punched Eddie in the arm.

"Ouch, fucker," Eddie said and punched him back.

Aaron ignored the punch and his brother and headed straight for the truck.

"But what does—?"

Aaron rounded back on Eddie. "Google is your friend, Ed. Use it."

He couldn't believe his older brother had just asked him sex questions. What was it with them all? He was a paramedic, with battlefield experience, not a counselor or a midwife, and certainly not an expert in marital sex with the due date eight weeks away.

"Why did Daddy punch you?" Milly asked.

"An' why did you punch him back?" Jake added.

"Your dad was playing a joke on me, and we didn't really hurt each other," Aaron explained and started the car.

I wish I could have. I'd have quite enjoyed pummeling Eddie into the ground now that he's all soft in the middle and complacent and I'm still at the gym and could take him down in an instant.

"I can't wait to canter." Milly changed the subject, chattering on about the horses and her hero Luke and the possibility they might go for a swim in Silver Lake after, and wasn't it great that her rabbits, Ginny and Harry, made babies like her stepmom and dad did.

Some of those things Aaron was cool with talking about, but the babies bit? He was steering clear of that one.

THEY MADE it to Crooked Tree a little after three, and on Sundays, the place was quieter. The guests who rented cabins were still there, but the walk-through visitors who were there for Sunday lunch at Branches would have moved on by now. He remembered coming here as a kid and it being empty, but with the push in marketing and the reputation for horse care, riding, and food at the restaurant, Crooked Tree was becoming something more than a dude ranch. It was *the* local place to go for a business meeting or a family outing. Walks along the river, watching the horses, the food, all of it was making the place valuable in the community, and wider.

"Uncle Aaron? Why are you dressed so fancy?" Milly asked.

Aaron parked the car at the end of a row, in the shade of the trees, and killed the engine.

"Fancy?" He attempted innocence, but he was lucky none of his brothers had called him on it. Ordinarily happy in jeans and T's with cute messages, he'd worn a button-down, with his best jeans. Like the kind of thing he'd wear on a night out. All that was missing was lube, condoms, and a ready smile.

"And you smell really nice," she pointed out.

"He put gunk on his hair too," Jake added and then snorted a laugh as he pressed his small hand to Aaron's hair and made a face.

Sue him, but if there was a chance of meeting Rob again today, he wanted to have his armor in place. It wasn't as if he wanted to act on his attraction. Looks aside, Rob was not his type, far too action-man, stubborn, and an asshole.

He caught Jake's hand and swung him onto his shoulders, not caring that his hair was getting messed up.

"Little man, one day you will want gunk in your hair for all the good reasons."

Jake clung to his head, laughing like a loon, and Milly skipped alongside him and around him, making him dizzy with her energy.

"Aaron's got a boyfriend. Aaron's got a boyfriend!" she singsonged as she danced, and he wasn't going to tell her to stop, because she was damn cute.

They walked up past Branches and the shop and on to the stables. Luke waved at them from the shade of the feed store. Milly ran the last few feet, and Luke swung her up and around before setting her down and grinning widely.

"How you doin' this weekend, Miss Milly?"

"We went swimming, and I swam all the way to the big rock, and so did Jake."

Luke ruffled her hair and lifted his arms to take Jake. "Wow, that's cool, and you're only six."

Milly smacked Luke's leg, and he made a show of hobbling.

"I'm older than that," she admonished, but she was grinning as well.

"Right you two, go find Pippa and Sky, and I'll be in there soon."

Luke let Jake down, and the two children raced away to find the horses, and Aaron watched them go, exchanging waves with Gabriel who was sitting at a desk writing. He'd keep an eye on them while Aaron had his weekly catchup with Luke.

"Milly says she wants to canter."

"She's ready for it, and for maybe moving up bigger than Pippa."

"Okay, but it's Jake you need to watch out for. He says he wants to go bouncing on the saddle."

Luke raised an eyebrow. "Message received. Talk later." He turned to leave, and generally, at this point, Aaron would either get a coffee at Branches or maybe watch the kids or wander around Crooked Tree. He had a solid hour of me-time, and he loved it. This week he had a specific goal in mind, though.

"Hey, Luke, you know Rob? He's staying here with two children. Says he's Justin's friend."

Luke went from confused to understanding. "Oh, the guy who's staying in the staff cabin? That Rob?"

"I guess so."

"What about him?"

"Nothing, just wanted to catch up with him."

Luke didn't question that, just gestured down the hill toward the staff places, which mostly sat empty now.

Not thinking too hard about what he was doing, he flattened his hair down again and sauntered to the bridge and over to the cabins. It was easy to spot which one Rob and his nephews were in, by the fact that the windows were open. He walked around the back of that one, not quite knowing what he was looking for.

Only when he saw Rob sitting on the back porch staring at the lake, he knew exactly what he'd hoped to find.

"What are you doing here?" Rob cut straight to the point.

"Just walking." Aaron moved to the porch steps and leaned against a post, one boot on the first step, the other flat on the ground.

"Then I suggest you walk away."

Nope, he was not walking away. He had questions, and a burning need to check the man out again. "Why are you in a staff cabin?"

Rob leaned forward in his chair. "I'm staff. Obviously. I clean the bathrooms. They make me use a toothbrush. It's unfair. You think I should I join a union?"

"Smartass."

"And I ask again. Why are you here, and why do you have your foot on my property?"

Aaron glanced down at his boot and smirked. "This?" he asked and hooked his thumbs in his belt loops.

"Move away."

"Before what? You get territorial on me?" He laughed then. "You got coffee in there?" He took another step up, so he was entirely on Rob's ground, and then he stopped and waited.

"Jesus," Rob said with a sigh. "You're not going, are you." It was a statement of fact and one that didn't need an answer. Rob headed inside. "Stay the fuck out there."

So Aaron did. He stayed with both feet on the porch, and after a few moments, he took the nearest seat, a large Adirondack with views of the mountain. He wondered where the children were. He couldn't hear talking or laughter, and to be honest, if his own niece and nephew spotted him, they would have been out here messing with him.

"Here." Rob thrust a coffee at him, and Aaron jumped a little.

"You're a ninja," he offered.

"Nah, you're just soft around the edges."

"I can't deny that," Aaron murmured. "Learning not to jump at the slightest thing is one of the things I've mastered that makes me a productive citizen."

"Is that what you are? All normal now?"

"Sometimes." Then he changed the subject. "Where are Bran and Toby?"

"Toby's napping. Bran watches over him; it's a sibling thing."

Aaron hesitated a little. "Do you think Bran seems very protective?"

"They're fine."

"I wasn't saying they weren't."

Rob huffed, and that was the end of that conversation. In silence, they sipped coffee, both staring at the same view.

"So, let's not fuck about here. Do you switch?" Aaron finally asked because as Nanna Carter had always said, *you don't ask you don't get.*

"What the hell?" Rob said.

Aaron sighed and finished his coffee. "Are we doing that, then?"

"Doing what?"

"Pretending we're not going to end up in bed with each other or screwing over the nearest surface." He patted the handrail that ran along the porch. "Or maybe you bent over here."

"I don't have time for your shit."

His expression belied his words. In fact, he checked Aaron out right there and then, his gaze lingering a long way south of Aaron's face.

Aaron tilted his hips a little and hooked the thumb of his left hand in a belt loop. "So you never answered my question about switching?"

Rob shot him a glance that spoke volumes. "Do you?"

Aaron didn't know where he was taking this, but he wanted *something* from Rob. He just hadn't decided what yet. He deliberately raked a look from head to toe, stopping halfway and nodding.

"I wouldn't say no…" He trailed off and raised his coffee mug in salute. "So, uncomplicated fucking or not?"

Rob placed his mug very carefully on the table, and Aaron waited for the explosion. They were two strong, determined; some would say stubborn, men, and who was to say they'd be compatible at all? It seemed that what they'd done so far was get up in each other's faces. He expected Rob to say something sarcastic so they could carry on this weird sexual thing they had going on, but all Rob did was stand, go into his cabin, and shut the door in Aaron's face.

Amused and turned on more than he liked to admit, Aaron left his mug on the step.

It was a damn shame Rob hadn't immediately agreed to his proposal, because the back view of Rob walking in the cabin was as damn fine as the front.

Chapter Six

ROB WASN'T GOING TO STAND THERE WITH HIS BACK TO THE
door, angsting over the fact he'd just turned down the sexiest
man he'd seen in, possibly, his entire life. That wasn't his
style. He could have said yes right there and then, got the itch
out of his system, and be done with it. But he had a list of
priorities, and hot sweaty sex was way down after getting the
children out.

Not to mention Aaron was connected to the ranch, and
Rob didn't want to complicate matters. He just wished his
libido understood the priorities because he was as hard as
freaking iron. He could almost imagine the taste of Aaron, the
scrap for control, the tussle they would have, and he groaned.

"Uncle Rob." Bran made him snap out of thoughts he had
no right to think.

Bran seemed as if he was going to cry. Or laugh. Or pee
his pants. Or something that Rob had no idea how to handle.
He was so serious, his face scrunched up, and hair in a wild,
spiky mess around his head. He had his hands on his hips,
and the stubborn expression reminded him so much of his

sister at that age that Rob rubbed at the quick pain which tightened in his chest.

"What's wrong?" Rob asked, placing his empty mug on the back of the counter, and even though his back protested, he crouched to Bran's level. Of course, then he was eye to eye with Bran, and he seemed even harder to read when he was at this angle.

"Toby is locked in the bathroom."

Okay. This he could handle. "You can turn the lock on the outside, let him out."

"I can't." A single tear rolled down Bran's face, and Rob felt desperate. Bran hadn't cried once since he picked them up and had no idea what he'd do if he did it for real. "He said I had to go away. He doesn't want me." He hiccupped a sob, and Rob reached out to touch a small shoulder, but Bran shrunk away from him.

He didn't need Rob touching him or offering comfort, and that was good because it would all be pretense anyway. He couldn't love the boys or keep them. He had to keep his heart hard.

"I'm sure he didn't mean that."

"*You* need to help him," Bran said. "It's uncle stuff now."

Rob nodded. Just because he opened the door didn't mean he'd have to talk to Toby or help him in any way. He didn't want either kid to get used to him being around, and helping them in the bathroom was a step too far. But unlocking a door? He could do that, professionally and effectively.

It took him a few seconds to work out that the lock was jammed, to use his penknife to ease the screw, and then jiggle it to get in. He was an expert at breaking into places that people didn't want him entering.

The door swung in, and he couldn't see Toby at first.

Then he heard the sobbing. Inside the bath, behind the shower curtain, a little boy was crying hard.

Now what?

"You need to check he's okay," Rob told Bran and waited for him to run to his brother's aid.

"No, you should," he countered.

Bran looked up at him as if Rob had suggested chopping the head off Toby's Bunny.

"He's upset," he informed Rob. "And he doesn't want me. He said so."

"I'm sure he didn't mean it. He's your brother."

"I'm not making him cry more." He crossed his little arms over his chest. The implication was that it was Rob's job to make Toby cry.

"But…" Rob wished he had an answer to that one. Then he sighed internally. What would it hurt to see what was upsetting the little man? Just because he fulfilled some small fatherly duty, didn't mean that Toby would form a secure attachment to him. The plan was to form zero attachments, which would make everything so much easier when he left them there and vanished.

Bran watched him, probably expecting him to fail miserably. Which he likely would.

Cautiously Rob walked in, his observation skills cataloging everything. The towel on the floor, Bunny dripping wet and covered in something very green. That would be shampoo, he thought, because there was a trail of the green stuff to a shampoo bottle, and it was smeared over the side of the bath. Then there was the fact that the towel rail was hanging on its side. How had one small boy done this much damage? He felt the burn of Bran's stare at his back and pushed the door closed a little to block the judgment. Then he sat on the side of the bath and gently pushed back the curtain.

Toby was curled in a little ball on his side, and the crying had stopped, but he had his arms over his head, and he was still in his pajamas.

"Hey Toby," Rob began, with what he hoped was his best considerate, don't-think-of-me-as-your-dad uncle voice. "What's up, buddy?" He waited for a detailed explanation, and one that would make sense of everything that was happening here.

"I peed on the floor," Toby said really quietly.

"That's okay, buddy. We've all done that in our time." There. That was the right thing to say. A mom might well make a joke about boys and missing the toilet, but Rob took this brotherhood of men thing very seriously, so no jokes.

"Then I put Bunny down, tried to wipe the pee with the towel, and it got stuck, and I yanked it, and the bar fell off, and I tripped, and the bottle fell over, an' it's all on Bunny, and I threw it…" His words grew slurred with new tears. Rob wondered if he should mention that Toby shouldn't really have wiped up pee with a towel, but what was the point. Bringing the kids up the right way wasn't his job.

"You want to know something? Once I peed on the floor, and I slipped in it and fell over," Rob lied.

Actually, it had been blood that had pooled on the floor after a particularly vicious takedown of a trio of men determined to bomb an office block in Fort Lauderdale. But, the falling over part was real.

"Did you break anything?" Toby asked after a small pause. At least he'd stopped crying, although he was snotty and wiped his face on his pajamas.

"What?"

"When you fell over."

"The sink, the towel rail, and my wrist," Rob said, and all

of that was true. It was the only bone he'd ever broken, and Justin had had to make up an elaborate cover story to take him to the hospital for X-rays and help.

Sometimes on cold, damp mornings, his wrist ached. A reminder of better times when the pain was something he could manage by sheer willpower alone.

"I shouted at Bran," Toby admitted, "but I didn't want him to see me make all this mess 'cos he would think we'd get in trouble."

"He knows you didn't mean it, Toby. So how about we get you in the shower, and I'll tidy up a bit."

"You'll fix it?"

"Of course." He should add something cute, like maybe mentioning that fixing things was what uncles did best. He didn't, because that would be stupidly dangerous.

"What about Bunny?"

"Maybe Bunny needs a shower," he said helpfully. More like a cycle in a washing machine, which he'd need to add to the list of things the boys would need from their new parents after he left.

Give them a homegrown family.

Get them into school.

Keep them happy.

Wash Bunny.

Then he tugged the curtain closed, assuming that Toby actually knew how to run the shower, waiting for it to begin. Only when Toby threw out his PJs and the scent of strawberry shower gel filled the bathroom did Rob relax into clearing up the mess. The towel rail was wrenched from the wall, so it would need fixing correctly, but who needed a rail for a towel anyway? That was why chairs and doors had been invented. So he eased out what remained of the second screw holding it and slid the rail down behind the toilet where it was out of the way.

After clearing up, he hovered just outside, his dormant uncle instincts poking at him, making him concerned about the little boy who might need him.

"I said he wanted you and not me. Told you," Bran said.

He could have meant anything, but Rob assumed Bran was commenting on how he'd done dealing with the situation. It was weird how good it felt getting a gold star from Bran Grady.

Wait, was Grady their last name? He'd never checked. Had the two of them kept his sister's last name, or were they something else? He opened the pack of information that Protection Services had given him, flicked through to find birth certificates. Both gave the father's name and the death certificate in there for his sister didn't mention a married name.

Okay, so they were both Grady, at least he knew that because hell, both of them were of school age, right? Maybe he wouldn't push it now. He'd wait until just before he left. Someone else, Justin maybe, would have to deal with the schooling side of things. He wouldn't have any choice when Rob faded into the night.

Since their arrival, things had moved fast. Justin had said one night, but Rob wasn't planning on leaving anytime soon, and they were at day two now. The cabin was big; a kitchen, a sitting area with huge sofas, and four bedrooms, the kids in the back rooms and him between them and the front door.

Old habits die hard.

A routine of eating breakfast at the table, then lunch and dinner up at Branches was set. They didn't talk a lot, the three of them, but he'd learned things about the kids in their silence.

Bran was the one who did all the thinking, and Toby was the emotional one who couldn't vocalize his pain. Not that Bran was that good at expressing pain as such, but he was an open book when he did have emotions. They didn't talk about their mom much, a few passing comments was all, and even though Rob had a few questions, he wasn't sure how to word them.

Was she a good mom? Had she ever wondered if he was still alive? Or was this thing where she'd wanted him to have the boys her way of saying that she'd known he was still out there? He'd cut all ties out of necessity, but had she been unhappy that he hadn't been there for her?

Am I sad I didn't see her? Was it worth missing out on having a sister just to save other people's families?

He pushed the questions aside and poured another coffee, checked the kids who were both sitting in front of the television, and then sauntered out to the back porch, part of him expecting Aaron to be there still.

Of course, he wasn't.

Justin had always talked about home, during their downtime when they'd run out of things to do and realized they weren't attracted to each other enough to even bother having sex. He described mountains and valleys and the river that ran through them. He talked about the lake he and the children had walked up to. Blue Lake? Green Lake? Something like that.

No, Silver. Silver Lake.

And horses. Justin had rambled on about horses one time when he'd had a post-op fever, about how he missed the horses and the ranch, and how much he hated himself for how his best friend had died and it was his fault.

It turned out he was wrong. Justin's best friend, Adam, hadn't died at all, but that didn't stop the guilt he could see consuming Justin at times. In their line of work, they couldn't feel guilt. They couldn't see the shades of gray at all. Things were black and white and had to stay that way. The bad guys were going to hurt innocent people, and he had been the good guy who cut out cancer before it hurt anyone else.

He didn't regret a single kill.

Not when it kept much better people than him safe. Suzi had been safe, so had Bran and Toby, because of him and Justin.

"Food!" he announced.

Watching Bran with Toby made him think back to what Aaron had hinted at, that Bran was maybe *too* concerned about his brother. All this time he'd thought his sister was safe, that the kids he knew she'd had were growing up happy. But was he wrong? He needed to talk to Justin or whoever finally agreed to take them, and tell him that Bran had to understand he wasn't Toby's parent. He had to be a little boy and stop worrying.

Something else to add to the list.

THE THREE OF them headed for Branches and only reached the bridge before Rob spotted his first target.

"Hi," he said and stepped in front of a tall, slim woman with long, dark blonde hair, who came to an abrupt halt and blinked at him. "Rob Brady, Justin's friend, and these rug rats are my nephews Bran and Toby. You're Ashley, right?"

She smiled at him and took his extended hand. "I am. Sorry I haven't been down to see you, but," she patted her swollen belly, "five months, and I'm on bedrest for blood pressure. Don't tell Gabe I'm out here."

Rob mimed zipping his lips, and she laughed. It was a nice laugh, and when she leaned over to talk to the children, he felt this overwhelming warm fuzziness that she would probably *love* to take them on and be their mom. Second choice after Justin and Sam, but still, a definite possibility.

"We're just going up to Branches to get food."

She frowned thoughtfully and glanced up at the restaurant, then brightened. "Try the chocolate fudge cake. It's a new recipe of mine. Let me know what you think."

"We sure will."

See, I can do the polite stuff.

"Do you like Crooked Tree?" she asked the children.

"It's cool for a holiday," Bran said, and Toby stayed quiet.

"It sure is," she said.

But all Rob heard was that Bran thought this was a holiday, and he needed to start building up the idea that this was a forever home for them, if he could work it all out. Ashley winked and moved away, and Rob carried on up the hill, following the kids.

"Did you like Ashley?" he asked in a special tone that didn't imply they had to like her.

"She has pretty hair," Toby murmured.

"It's really long."

"I bet it's soft."

"Like Mom's," Bran said.

Then they fell quiet again, and both of them stopped dead, right in front of him. He wondered if they were going to cry. He should hug them, and tell them everything was going to be okay. Only he couldn't, because it wasn't going to be okay for them, not yet.

Chapter Seven

AARON COULDN'T GET HIS MIND OFF THE TALL, DARK, dangerous guy who'd shut the door in his face. Not at home, and certainly not at work when they were in a lull. He'd had one or two very vivid daydreams about what he'd like to do to Rob if he ever got his hands on him.

"What is this!" Grace snapped and thrust her phone into his face. He couldn't focus on it and worried if he moved said phone would give him a concussion.

"What am I looking at?"

Grace waggled the phone and scowled at him. "Oh I don't know, maybe a Facebook group called 'who's the daddy?' A group *you're* a member of, asshole."

Wait. How would she know that? The group was secret. Aaron realized too late that it was *his* phone she was shaking at him and lunged for it. She was too fast, scooping it back and pushing it into her pocket. "You left it in the cab, and I saw an update, so spill, Carter," she ordered.

He could tackle her right here and now, get the phone back, and pretend he knew nothing, but she was pregnant, seemed pissed, and he feared for the survival of his cellphone and his balls.

He decided to go for cute. It worked most of the time.

"In my defense, it wasn't my idea, and also you were never meant to find out about the group."

"That is a shit defense, Carter."

"I know."

"Exactly whose idea was it?"

Aaron raised his hands. "I swore an oath—" he let out an *oof* as she smacked him upside the head.

"You're an idiot, and I don't know why we're friends, but tell me, why the hell would someone put both Chris Pratt *and* Chris Evans as options for the dad?"

Aaron opened his mouth to answer, but she cut him off.

"Don't bother." She tossed the phone to him. "Why is it everyone is so damn interested in who the father of my baby is, anyway?"

Aaron had a lot of answers for that. The mystery of Grace's baby's daddy was bound to engender interest, and the question that everyone discussed was why she wouldn't just come out and tell everyone. Then there was the fact that Grace didn't seem herself at all, quite apart from being pregnant and tired. Maybe it was only him who noticed the times she seemed lost, and the moments he caught her staring into the distance.

"You know what this place is like," he offered lamely because that seemed like the safest bet.

She slumped to sit next to him, legs sprawled, and leaned on his shoulder, and for a few moments, they sat quietly.

"It's complicated," she said.

"You know I'm here if you need to talk," he offered and then waited for her to turn around and say it was none of his business. They might be partners, riding the ambulance together, but at the end of the day, this was clearly something serious that she wasn't ready to share. At first, he thought maybe it was because she'd considered whether to keep the baby, but no, she'd very clearly told everyone she was pregnant and added how excited she was.

"I'm not sure people would understand. Not even you." She added the last part softly, but he heard it.

"You could try me."

"I was seeing someone. They decided to finish things. They broke my heart, told me I needed to sort my life out and see someone my own age. I sulked for two months, then one night, I went mad, ended up sleeping with a guy whose name I don't even know. Once, Aaron, and now look at me."

She snuggled into his side and buried her face in his sleeve, and for a moment when she stared up at him, he thought she was going to say something else. But like every part of his damn life, the emergency call coincided with her open expression, and then they were rushing to attend, and there was no time to share anything.

They dealt with two calls back-to-back. The first, and easiest, was a ten-year-old falling out of a tree. The kid had been retrieving a balloon, and there had been a clean break in his femur. The second was way more complicated, and was a call that left both Aaron and Grace subdued after.

They'd both known the patient, Michaela Langdon, and finding her dead from an overdose from the pills scattered around her was a shock. It was widely known that she had breast cancer, but last Aaron knew she was fighting it and had been in remission. Maybe something had happened, bad news from the hospital, or had she just been tired?

"She was the same age as Saul, fifty-four. He was at school with her," Aaron said as the two of them sat in the ambulance in the parking lot after their shift.

Grace stared at him in shock, like it hadn't occurred to her how old Michaela was.

"I only saw her last week," she murmured. "She was going to make a blanket for the baby. I never saw anything in her that made me think…"

Aaron wanted to say that he'd seen this before. On occasion, he could see when someone was on edge, knew that they were going to take their own lives. Other times there was no sign. He'd seen too many veterans eat bullets ever to think that he could tell just by looking at someone what their mental state was.

"Sometimes you just can't tell," he said.

They went their separate ways, but Aaron didn't head home. Instead, he stood on the corner of Main and debated what to do next. Left took him to Carter's and his brother, Saul. Right took him to his car and up to Crooked Tree.

Why the hell was he debating going up to Crooked Tree? He certainly wasn't going to visit the horses, and the man who was taking up way too many of his thoughts had shut the door on him, and that had to be a sign that he just wasn't interested in Aaron.

Carters it was, because Saul should hear the news about Michaela from him, and he strode down the road with purpose, letting himself through the back and heading straight for the kitchen. It was three in the afternoon, and that meant one thing. Saul would be cooking. Carters offered a limited menu, mostly for drinkers late in the evening, bar snacks, that kind of thing. But it was all handmade by Saul, and there was a comfort in knowing exactly where to find him as he prepared it all.

He should tell Saul about Michaela dying. It would mean something to him, and he thought carefully about how he would word it. Saul was stirring chili, lost in thought when Aaron walked in the door.

"Hey, big brother," he announced his arrival and went straight to the fridge, taking out a beer.

"Shoes!" Saul barked without even turning around. Jason always said their oldest brother had eyes in the back of his head, but Aaron knew it was just that all of them were predictable in all the stupid things they did, and Saul, as the surrogate parent, just knew what they were like.

"Already done it," Aaron lied and toed his sneakers off before Saul turned around and saw he was lying, even though he bet Saul knew he was lying. Beer in hand, he moved next to Saul, wondering how to explain what had happened.

Saul side-eyed him and frowned. "Shit day, eh?"

"Not a good one," Aaron began.

Saul must have seen something in his expression, and he laid down the spoon he'd been using. "What? What is it? Is it Grace, is everyone okay?"

How the hell did he word this? He'd told families about the death of loved ones before, and he'd had all the right training. But this was his big brother, and Michaela had been his friend for a long time. "We had a call to Michaela Langdon's place. She's taken her own life."

There, he'd said it, ripped off the Band-Aid, and then stood, ready to be the support that Saul might need. He and Michaela had a friendship from school, but in a small town like this, that friendship had never gone away but had grown into them knowing each other's business. She'd have been one of the friends who didn't query why eighteen-year-old Saul was ready to give everything up to care for his four brothers. When she'd come back from college, she had been a solid support to Saul in the early years.

Saul was pale, stepped back from the stove, and sat

heavily on the nearest chair. He scrubbed at his face, and his eyes were bright with emotion.

"Shit," he muttered. "That was why she…"

Aaron got another beer from the fridge and sat opposite Saul, nudging the bottle toward him.

"What?" he asked.

"She was here two days ago, handed over all these recipes she'd been given by her mom. I should have known something was wrong because she refused to share them with me all these years, but she was adamant I take them, and then she hugged me. I asked her if she was okay, and she said everything was great. I thought she meant she was still clear of cancer."

Aaron sighed. "I checked in with Doc Logan. He couldn't tell me much just that the cancer had returned, aggressively. She'd been given the option of treatment to extend her life a few more months. I guess she decided to go out her own way."

Tears collected in Saul's eyes, and he raised his beer.

"Michaela," he offered a toast, his words thick with grief.

"Michaela," Aaron repeated, and they clinked bottles.

"Life is too short," Saul said and picked at the label on his beer. "We fuck everything up, and then we die."

"That's not true," Aaron defended. "What about living for now and making the most of things."

"When you get in your fifties, then you'll see. We're all so old now."

"You're only fifty-four. That's not old. Cancer is a crap shoot, Saul. Doesn't mean it'll take us all."

Saul swallowed some beer and coughed, then changed the subject. "Her kids will be devastated," he said. "Imagine losing their mom like that. Hell, Katie is in Japan studying, and Johnny is still at college." He bowed his head. "Guess they'll both come home for the funeral, put their mom to rest."

Aaron allowed Saul a few moments of reflection, but then instinct kicked in. They needed to remember the good things about Michaela.

"You remember when I was thirteen, and she came over with Johnny when he was only little, and Eddie decided to play hide and seek only he got bored, and Johnny stayed in the bath behind the shower curtain for an hour."

"I remember Michaela chasing Eddie around the garden with a broom."

"And that time that…"

They exchanged stories; they remembered. But Michaela had been Saul's friend, and it was he who spoke the most. At first, his voice would crack when he revealed the little things that made up a friendship, but then he became stronger. By the time the bar outside was filling, and he had to work, he seemed more even. But he did add something cryptic to the end, when he was staring into his coffee cup. "I'm right to think about my age."

"I'll man the bar," Aaron offered after seeing his brother so sad.

Saul shook his head. "No, I need this. We'll all raise drinks to her."

Aaron stayed for an hour and then left, knowing that somehow, in all of this, Saul would be okay.

Then he didn't know what to do with himself. He felt restless and antsy and headed for Hepburn House, changing his mind as he drew closer. Being there wasn't what he needed. He knew what he *really* wanted, and he headed up the mountain and directly for Crooked Tree.

When he turned into the parking area, the clock on his dash showed it was six p.m., and he considered whether he should get something from Branches, given he hadn't eaten since breakfast, and that had been a donut he'd stolen from the night shift. The thought of Sam's cooking was enough to have him heading to the restaurant first, and as if fate had planned it, Rob, Bran, and Toby were sitting at a table with menus in front of them. Pulling back his shoulders, he headed their way, knowing Rob had spotted him, and then slid into the fourth chair, reaching over to steal a menu from the table next to them.

"What's the special?" he asked as if it was perfectly fine to have just joined the small family.

Rob stared at him, his eyes narrowing a little, and so much unspoken passed between them.

You're an asshole, Rob was likely thinking, with an added *fuck right off.*

The waitress came over, took the kids' orders, and then waited.

"Steak, rare. Fries, salad. Thank you," Rob ordered.

"Make that two," Aaron said and then waited for the explosion from Rob, just as he did every single time he talked to him. One day it would happen, and it would be delicious as hell to face off against him. *One day* Aaron would push Rob too far, and then that would be it. That was the moment they could fuck each other's brains out and get it out of their system. But there was nothing. In fact, he deliberately ignored Aaron. He didn't know why he wanted that fiery anger from Rob tonight. Maybe it was seeing an old family friend die. Maybe it was remembering Rob refusing to leave the car? All Aaron knew was that he was needy right *now*.

"How long are you staying here?" Aaron asked him, to get a conversation going. He couldn't help but notice both children looking at their uncle as if they wanted to know the answer as well.

"We're not sure," Rob answered after a moment's hesitation.

Aaron shifted in his seat, knocked his foot against Rob's, and then deliberately left it there. He pushed again. "You must have some idea?"

"Uncle Rob says it's a holiday," Bran piped up, but there was a question in his tone. Rob ignored him, made a show of studying the menu, even though they'd all ordered.

"Is it a long vacation?" Aaron wanted something from Rob, confirmation, denial, anything more than the vague shit he was handing out about everything.

Rob put his menu down. "Can we talk?"

He asked *oh so damn politely*, but Aaron didn't have to be an expert to see the flash of temper.

"Sure," Aaron said

"Stay here, kids. We'll be back in five."

Aaron felt a swell of lust inside at the five-minute thing. He and Rob could expend a lot of energy in five minutes. Rob left the restaurant, and Aaron followed him out and back around the restaurant and into the trees. He didn't even see Rob move until he was shoved against the nearest tree and pinned there. The strength in Rob was precisely what he needed, the tough body pressed against him, and he was hard in an instant.

"I don't have time for your shit," Rob growled, pressing harder. If he expected Aaron to stand still, he was in for a surprise because Aaron had moves of his own. In a second, their positions were reversed.

"Now it's my turn," he said, his grip just as tight, and feeling Rob hard against him. Lust hung around them. "We need to clear the air here. A fuck might help."

Rob did some clever shit with his feet, and Aaron ended

up on his back, with Rob crouched over him, gripping Aaron's balls. "Are you an imbecile?"

Aaron smirked. "You gonna move your hand? Get me off here?"

Rob looked down at where his hand was, as if he hadn't realized what he was even doing, and he released his hold before sitting back on his haunches.

"Rob?"

"You are a fucking asshole."

"Back at you."

Rob sighed noisily. "We can't do this. I *can't* do this."

"But you want to, right? You need me to say the words, huh? I want my hands on you. I want you on your knees with my cock in your mouth. Here. Now."

Rob backed away. "I can't."

"There's no such thing as can't."

"You're dangerous," Rob muttered after a moment's silence.

Aaron watched him leave, but then followed him. He could work with *I can't*. They sat back at the table opposite each other as if they hadn't just grappled on the ground. And sue him, but he pushed his foot against Rob's and left it there.

"Did you fight?" Bran gripped Toby's hand and stared right at Rob.

"No."

The answer was short, and there was no affection in Rob's tone, no further explanation to reassure his nephew.

"Not at all," Aaron said because kids needed comfort. He didn't know why Rob was an asshole. "Sometimes grown-ups need to discuss things where children can't hear because we curse a lot."

"Oh that," Bran said, all matter of fact. "Uncle Rob curses in front of us all the time."

"I don't," Rob defended.

He probably did, but luckily dinner arrived, and the subject was changed. Aaron kept up a conversation with the children; they reminded him of his niece and nephew. He watched Rob's expression throughout the meal. At first, Rob was impassive and not part of the conversation at all, but soon he became thoughtful, and not for the first time, Aaron wondered what was going on behind his eyes. There was something else in that hard expression; sadness maybe?

I don't need to know the man to screw his brains out.

"So Rob," he said as they finished off ice cream for dessert. "Back to yours for coffee?"

He couldn't fail to see the way Rob turned and stared at him, so he met that gaze head-on.

Do you want this? Aaron tilted his head, even as he knew he couldn't ask that question in front of the kids.

"I don't think so. We need to go," Rob said but didn't take his eyes off Aaron. "Coffee will have to be another day," he added. He seemed torn, as if he hadn't meant to say that, or was it just Aaron being over optimistic? There was *something* between them, a spark, and hadn't he said that he wanted Aaron? That Aaron was dangerous?

What was stopping Rob? Was it the children? Was it Aaron himself? Was it something to do with the pain Rob was obviously in or the flash of uncertainty in his expression?

The man was intriguing, unsettling, gorgeous. All Aaron wanted to do was talk to him and find out what made him tick. It had been a long time since a man had impacted him like this. So many years in the army, and outside of his one relationship with Elijah, he was resigned to being the proud owner of several superficial hookups.

Of course, catting around when he was off duty had stopped with Elijah. He hadn't had anything since then, not a connection, not making love, nothing. Hell, he and his right hand had a very close relationship.

Maybe that is why you're obsessed with Rob. Perhaps this is an entirely physical pheromone type thing.

He sat back in his seat, watched the small Brady family leave, ordered more coffee, and thought about what time the kids would be in bed.

Then he could visit Rob. Just to talk.

Obviously.

Chapter Eight

Rob didn't take the kids directly back to the cabin. Instead, he walked them around the side and knocked on the door that opened to the stairs to Justin and Sam's apartment above the restaurant. Sitting with Aaron at dinner had just reminded him of everything he couldn't have and the reason why he was at Crooked Tree.

Enough messing around, Rob.

He needed to find a family for Bran and Toby. Fantasizing about no-holds-barred sex was not the way to do that.

Focus.

There was no answer to his knock, but Rob had seen Justin go around this way only twenty minutes before and hadn't seen him come back. Added to that, Sam wasn't behind the counter of Branches, so he assumed they'd be together. Of course, he might be interrupting sexy times, but he had Bran and Toby to think of. He still hadn't pinned down Sam and Justin in one place to get to know them. They needed to see what good kids the boys were and that they'd fit into the Crooked Tree extended family well.

"What are we doing here?" Bran asked and kicked at a stone on the doorstep that led to the apartment entrance.

"Visiting."

Bran sighed like the put-upon eight-year-old he was. "We don't want to be here. Anyway, Toby is tired."

"No, I'm not," Toby defended. He did seem tired, but Rob was amazed because that was the first time he'd spoken for himself in direct opposition to his brother.

"Yes, you are," Bran said and tried to take his hand.

Toby stepped away. "Am not."

"You are."

"I'm not—"

"Guys, cool it a little, okay?" Rob interrupted the standoff. "No arguing, or you won't get the cookies that Sam always has in his place." The lie about the cookies was enough to get them to stop sniping, although Toby was as mutinous as a five-year-old could get, and Bran was glancing everywhere except at his brother. Rob knocked again, praying to anyone who listened that Sam or Justin would open the damned door before he had to break up sibling issues. Still nothing.

So he knocked again. And again. Louder each time.

And finally, he heard steps on the stairs.

"Something had better be on fire!" Sam called through the door, then swung it open violently. He was disheveled, his hair standing on end, his jeans unbuttoned, shirtless, and there was stubble burn on his face.

Yep, we totally interrupted their alone time. I should feel guilty, but I don't.

"Rob?" Sam looked down at the boys and then back up at Rob. "Is something wrong?"

"No, we just thought we'd visit," Rob said cheerfully. He knew better than to expand on the reasons. Keep the story simple, don't give Sam a chance to turn them away. Okay, so guilt was front and center at his lack of transparency, but he had to be hard here. This was the best chance for a home for Bran and Toby.

Don't apologize because that shows you accept you've interrupted.

"Uhm, okay." Sam glanced behind him up the stairs, then back at Rob. He was doing a lot of that, clearly off-balance.

"Yeah," Rob prompted and waited.

"You want to come in?" Sam asked finally.

Rob smiled then. "We'd love to. We hear you have a constant supply of cookies." He watched Sam blink at him as if he wasn't following the conversation. "The kids love cookies."

"Toby's too tired for a cookie," Bran snapped and crossed his arms over his chest.

"Am not!" Toby shouted back and, thank the heavens, Sam seemed to take pity on them. Either that, or he didn't know what the hell else to do.

"Come in. I have cookies," he announced and stepped back from the door. He went up first, taking the steps two at a time. "Justin! We have company!"

"Who the fu—?" Justin appeared at the top of the stairs and cut off his curse when he spotted the children. "What's wrong?"

Was that everyone's default setting around here, or was it just when it was anything to do with Rob?

Rob reached the top of the stairs, herding Bran and Toby before him, until they were all in the small sitting room, with the kitchen through an arch in the corner and a bedroom beyond an open door.

Justin went over and shut the bedroom door, then turned to Rob and waited. Rob shrugged because he hadn't thought this far ahead, not really. They were in the house, and this was the point Bran and Toby showed what fabulous kids they were and how easy it would be for Sam and Justin to take them in. So why did he feel so stupid that everything had gone to plan?

Isn't that what I want?

"Sit, please," Sam said and shoved cushions onto the floor, making room for Rob. "Bran, Toby, you want some milk with the cookies?"

At least Bran didn't kick off about Toby and what he thought his brother didn't need right now, and Toby simply nodded with enthusiasm, albeit somewhat sleepily.

He and Justin couldn't exactly talk there; but he had some things to get sorted out, the first being his weapon. So he didn't sit but walked the short distance to Justin.

"Do you have a lockbox you can store my gun in?" he asked under his breath.

Justin's eyes widened. "What?"

"I don't want the kids to get hold of it."

"And it's taken you all this time to ask me?"

"I had it out of reach and under control."

"You had a weapon at Crooked Tree? All this time?"

Rob lifted an eyebrow in silent condemnation of the comment. Of course he would be armed. He bet Justin was still carrying around a weapon, and he sure as hell knew there were rifles on the ranch.

Justin muttered another curse, and pushed open the bedroom door. "In here," he ordered, and Rob followed at a more leisurely pace. As soon as he was in, Justin shut the door again and then locked it before opening the closet and pressing a button to reveal a fake wall.

"Sam doesn't even know the code," Justin advised as he entered it into the lockbox before pressing his thumb to a pad.

The box *snicked* open, revealing two pistols, a Sig P226, and a Glock. Rob recognized them. Justin had been damn handy with the Glock, and it had been his pride and joy.

"When was the last time you used one of this?"

"That's none of your fucking business," Justin snapped. Then he closed his eyes briefly. "Not since Sam," he murmured and then stepped back to allow Rob into the space.

Rob pulled his own gun out, twirling it on his fingers, the movement familiar, then checked it was empty, slipping the bullets in there alongside Justin's and placing his weapon on top. Without ceremony, he shut the lid and heard the locks connect instantly.

"Don't tell me the code." Rob didn't want to see the gun again. He wasn't leaving this world putting a bullet in his brain. He was going to fall asleep and never wake up.

"What?"

How did he get Justin to understand he was done as much as Justin was? Not in the same way, not by choice at first, but he had other things to do in the next month or so than use a weapon on anyone. So he manned up and placed a hand on Justin's shoulder.

"The kids are my kryptonite," he said. "What Sam is to you," he began. "The reason I've stopped."

Justin softened a little. "Really?" He was asking for the truth from Rob, and he would know if Rob was lying. Maybe he was the only one in life who would.

Rob just needed to make sure of something first. "If anything happened to you, J, I would be there for Sam. You know that, right?"

There was that frown again, marring Justin's expression, as if he was waiting for the lies to drop and not fully understanding what Rob was saying. Then it became something more; raw, naked fear.

"What did you do, Rob? You said there was no danger!"

"No. Shit, no. I promise you there's nothing wrong. It's not that. It's just if you got ill, or you got hit by a car, you know I'd drop everything."

Justin crossed his arms over his chest, and his lips thinned. "And even if we could find you to help us, what would you do for Sam? Kill the illness for him? Shoot the driver of the car? Hug him?"

The words hurt because they were true. "I'd be proactive. I'm not exactly the hugging type."

"That's much is true."

"Bran and Toby are everything to me now, my complete focus." He wasn't lying. He didn't have anything else left to worry about.

"I can see those boys mean something to you." Justin admitted, almost reluctantly.

Rob wanted to say that doing that was out of character, that he didn't want to connect with Bran or Toby, that he was done, but that didn't fit the narrative he was trying to go for. He needed to convince Justin that the boys meant something to him. Then when the end came, Justin would feel responsible for them, and they would have him to turn to.

Sam knocked on the door and called out, and Justin pushed back the false sliding wall and then closed the closet.

They didn't speak as they walked out, but he saw Sam's concerned gaze and knew that there would be some talking between him and Justin when they were alone.

"You left us with him," Bran accused, and Rob took in the full picture. Bran and Toby, holding hands, standing by the small table, and staring at him angrily. Yeah, even Toby, and that was a new thing. The cookies were on the table, along with two glasses of milk, and it seemed as if the "leaving them alone with Sam" thing hadn't gone well.

"I was just inside with—"

"He tried to lift up Toby!" Bran shouted, which only caused Toby to hiccup a sob.

Sam was flustered. "I didn't mean to upset him. I was just helping him onto the high stool. I'm sorry—"

"We don't know him!" Bran sounded hysterical. "And you left us! We want to go back to the cabin."

Sam and Rob exchanged quick glances, and Sam seemed at a loss. Pretty much how Rob had felt since picking the boys up. This was not good.

He tried to calm the situation down. "Let's eat the cookies and—"

"Toby needs to go to bed." Bran was mutinous, his thin shoulders drawn back as if he would take on everyone in the room just to keep his brother safe. Did he not think that Rob could keep them safe? If it came to it, Rob could take Sam down in a second. Justin would take longer of course, and there *was* the whole thing with Rob's back.

"Uncle Rob!" Bran's demand cut into his deliberations, and with a quick look of apology to Sam, he and the boys left.

By the time they got back to the cabin, all three of them were in a mutinous silence. Bran wouldn't let go of Toby's hand, Toby was trying to yank free, and Rob? He followed and knew that he was completely fucked. There was more to Bran and Toby's story than he was aware of. This wasn't just about protecting a little brother.

"Can I talk to you, Bran?"

"No, Toby is tired."

Bran didn't even check him, following Toby into their room and shutting the door.

I should go in. I need to find out what has happened. Why is Bran so scared? Rob was sick at the assumptions he couldn't help but make. He lasted about thirty minutes, when all was peaceful and then quietly opened the door. Toby was fast asleep, Bunny wrapped in his arms, but Bran sat bolt upright in bed, staring at the door as if he'd known that Rob would go in. Rob sat on the end of the bed and didn't know where the hell to start.

"Did someone hurt you? After your mom died, when you were looked after?" he asked.

Bran tipped his chin, a mutinous expression on his face. "No. Because no one can hurt us. I won't let them. Not even you."

Another layer of hardness eased inside Rob. His nephew was so strong and brave, watching out for his little brother, facing off against Sam, refusing to allow the world to hurt them. He still had questions.

"Did someone make you think you had to be like that? Did someone hurt you?" he persisted, feeling so out of his depth. He needed a child psychologist. Or at least a member of the family he was leaving the boys with. Maybe he should go and get Ashley. Might they respond better to her than to Sam and Justin?

"I said no. Anyway, no one cares anyway. You didn't find us or care what happened to us," Bran stated. "But they made us go with you anyway so they didn't care either."

Bran lay down then, turning his back to Rob and snuggling close to Toby. Rob had this weird feeling that Toby was Bran's own kind of Bunny, easing his worries, keeping him calm.

Christ, this is all so freaking convoluted.

Rob sat for a while. Wasn't he caring by wanting to provide a home for them? Wasn't he showing that they meant something to him by finding them a forever family? Of course, they wouldn't realize that until he was gone, but they didn't need him to care. They needed someone else here to care.

"I do care," Rob murmured, and he wasn't lying. For the first time ever in his adult life he was thinking about the place in his heart where love was kept. He saw a slight shift of the covers, indicating that Bran had heard him. "Good night, Bran."

He left them, shut the door the way they always wanted, and dug his notebook out of his backpack. Writing this down might make sense, and he wrote down the names of the potential parents. Sam and Justin were still at the top of the list. He and Justin had a connection, and he would feel obligated to help. That much Rob knew. Also, they were good people, clearly in love, and hell, Sam must be strong to be able to hold Justin at night and chase away his demons. Their apartment wasn't big, but this cabin was permanently empty by all appearances, so there was no reason Sam and Justin couldn't be parents in here.

Then there was Gabe and Ashley, two children already, one on the way, but she was lovely, and Gabe seemed a strong, steady, devoted husband. Nate and Jay were on his periphery as well. They were already uncles, and the boys would slot in very well.

He added therapy to the list. Because, hell, there were things wrong here, and him leaving would make everything worse.

Unless they hate you, then they will be glad you're leaving.

When he'd finished writing it all down, the picture was better than he'd been thinking. One of those couples would have the boys, and then he could leave and find his own way to make things right for himself. The doctors had said three months. He'd already used up a month. Rolling his neck, he felt the satisfying crack and then pulled a soda from the fridge, determined to decompress.

Did it surprise him to find Aaron sitting on his back porch? Probably not. He'd been half expecting him to arrive all day.

"What are you doing here?"

Aaron stood. "Been thinking about this all day," he said, then covered the short distance between them and gripped the back of Rob's neck, tilting it a little and then kissing him, pushing him back, hard, against the wall of the cabin, so forcefully that pain spiked up Rob's spine. He could tell Aaron to cool it, or go with the flow, and fuck, he was already turned on, conditioned to lust as soon as he laid eyes on the man. So he switched their positions to ease the pressure on his spine, and it was him pushing Aaron against the wood, deepening the kiss, with Aaron gripping his hair and yanking his head back forcefully, biting his neck, then soothing it with his tongue.

"You wanna take this inside? I'll hold my hand over your mouth, so you're quiet."

Rob wasn't taking what they had anywhere near where the kids slept. He wanted Aaron as he wanted a random guy in a club. He wanted hard and fast and desperate, and he wanted it *now*. But he also wanted nasty and sordid and all the things that defined his quick hookups.

"No," Rob snapped, "not inside."

Chapter Nine

AARON'S LUST TURNED UP A NOTCH.

Grabbing Aaron's shirt, Rob pulled him away from the cabin, down the steps and into the trees to the left, shoving him against the nearest tree. Aaron wasn't going to let Rob run this, and gripped his top, pushing it up, getting his hands on soft, warm skin, and scraping his nails over hard nipples. Rob hissed, pressed closer, trapping Aaron's fingers between them, but Aaron wasn't a lightweight, and he wanted to move, damn it. He shoved, Rob shoved, and then they were kissing again.

This wasn't gentle or loving. This was raw need and power, and he twisted one hand in Rob's hair and held on for dear life. The kiss was aggressive, but the taste of Rob was intoxicating, the way he pushed for more, then gentled his tongue so that it took Aaron by surprise. He reached between them, working one-handed on Rob's jeans, slipping the buttons until he could get where he wanted; his fingers wrapped around Rob's cock.

Rob groaned, and the kiss was breathless and hard and focused. He thrust up into the circle of Aaron's hold.

Elation slammed into Aaron. He was getting this man off in the darkness, and he wanted to feel, but Rob was making no moves to return the favor, and Aaron's cock hurt.

He wanted to fight, to demand that Rob touch him, and he tried another direction. He untwisted his grip from Rob's hair then traced his back to the top of his ass, pushing his hand inside his shorts and grabbing the meaty globe of his ass, even as he twisted his other fingers on Rob's cock.

"Fuck," Rob groaned, pressing forward and then yanking himself away completely.

Aaron reached for him, but Rob sidestepped the hold before gripping Aaron's arm and making him turn so he faced the tree. Aaron braced himself, and Rob forced a hand into Aaron's pants, opening buttons and shoving the material down around his thighs, his shorts with it. Then Rob pushed against Aaron, his cock sliding between his butt cheeks, and gripped in Aaron's hand. For a short while, he rutted there, and Aaron circled his own cock. He didn't care how he got off, but it was damned nice to get off with Rob pressing against his ass.

"Don't touch," Rob growled and reached around to grasp Aaron's cock. He held and twisted and rutted, and Aaron was lost, pushing back against the tree. The noises they were making were muted. Both of them were clearly enough in the moment to know they were outside where anyone could hear them. When orgasm hit Aaron, he let out a cry of relief into Rob's hold, and Rob followed soon after, fucking into his hand and leaning over Aaron.

Silently Rob stepped away, pulling up his jeans, leaving them unbuttoned. This wasn't about reaching for a post-fuck kiss. This was nothing like affection or romance. This was getting off.

"Get the fuck away from me," Rob murmured and left.

He walked away without a backward glance, went into the cabin, and shut the door.

Aaron should've felt like he did after club hookups, sated but dirty.

He was sated. But he didn't feel dirty at all. If anything, he wanted more of what just happened. In a bed or at least in the light so he could see Rob's expression when he came.

Because he bet it was all kinds of hot.

AARON COULDN'T SHAKE the encounter. It stayed with him through his next shift, and even Grace called him on his inattention to the real word.

"Watch what you're doing, Aaron." She frowned and took the sanitization spray off him. "You sprayed that three times. I think it's done. What's wrong with you?"

He could've asked her the same question. She'd been quiet all morning and irritable. Which wouldn't matter normally, but grabbing breakfast at Carters before the start of the shift had him experiencing Saul in a bad mood as well. Aaron put that down to Michaela, and offered sympathy, but Saul had grunted that it was nothing to do with Michaela, and everything to do with being old and tired.

"I met this guy." Aaron decided to tell Grace. "And the sex was scorching."

Grace said she lived vicariously through his encounters and usually wanted all the details. But today all she did was stare at him.

"Well, there you go. You got sex. Well done you. And that caps my shitty day." She left the bus, and he followed her all the way to the ladies' restrooms and stood outside the door.

And waited. She didn't expect him to be there and glared at him when she walked out.

"Wait up. Grace, what's wrong?"

She turned to face him, and she was crying. Aaron was worried, and made to pull her into his arms, but she refused to be held and backed away. Their shift was over, and he didn't chase her.

Hormones probably. Had to be.

When his phone rang and it was Eddie, he didn't want to answer it but he did because hell, Eddie was his brother, and as much as he didn't want another conversation about Eddie's sex life, he couldn't avoid him.

"Shit, A, there's something wrong," Eddie said without preamble.

Instinct kicked in. This wasn't Eddie's whiny voice. This was his terrified-the-world-was-ending voice.

"What?"

"There's blood."

"Call 911," Aaron said.

"She won't let me. She says it's too early, I called you."

"I'll be there in five." He hung up and headed straight for the bus. He was off duty, but this was family. He caught up with Grace in the parking lot.

"Jenny's not good," he called. He didn't ask her to go with him. That was her decision to make, but was relieved when she climbed into the bus and belted up.

"Let's go," she said.

They made it to Eddie's place, not far from Carters, in less than three minutes, parked and were out of the ambulance immediately. Saul was at the door. He stopped Aaron with a touch to his arm.

"I think the baby is coming early," he said.

"Got it," Aaron confirmed and headed inside. He didn't

have to examine Jenny to know that things were advanced, too far gone for them to get her to hospital. She was curled up in pain on the floor of the front room, her skin pale, and her features screwed up with pain.

Eddie was frantic. "She started to bleed, and then the pain was so quick we didn't have time to... we couldn't... she wouldn't move—"

Aaron stopped Eddie from talking with a gentle hand to his chest. "I've got this, Eddie, let me fix things."

Eddie backed off, and Aaron immediately went to Jenny, Grace right by him.

"I can't get my hair up," Jenny said and cried out as pain doubled her over. "It's in my face. I hate it." She writhed and then stared up at Eddie. "I hate you," she said, panting through the last of the pain.

In a quick movement, Grace had Jenny's long, raven-black hair up in a messy ponytail, extricating the tie Jenny had gripped in her hand. "All done," she announced and held Jenny's hand as Aaron did checks.

"You're eight centimeters," he announced.

"I can't be!" Jenny snapped.

"The baby isn't due for another four weeks," Eddie interjected and went to hold his wife's other hand. "This is all my fault," he added, broken, and stared right at Aaron.

"A baby coming early is no one's fault," Aaron said firmly and eased Jenny back against the pile of cushions Eddie had made. "Okay, Jenny, I need you to breathe through the next contraction for me."

"Towels, hot water," Grace demanded, and Saul moved quickly to gather what Aaron needed.

Aaron could feel the rippling of her belly, the movement below his fingers. There was no time to get her to the hospital. He was going to have to deliver this baby right now in his brother's front room. Listening for the heartbeat, it sounded strong, and then Jenny screamed when a contraction tore through her.

This was too fast. This wasn't the slow labor that women hoped for, no gas and air, or an epidural. This was nasty and violent, and Aaron put on his game face. He'd seen blood before, he'd seen pain before, and now he needed to focus on the baby and mom.

The baby was head down, thank god, and he didn't have to do a thing. With a final push from Jenny, his niece arrived in the world, pale and gray, but at least the cord wasn't wrapped around her neck. She was a good size and breathing on her own. He cleared the airways, checked the heart, wrapped her in one of the clean towels, and handed her to Jenny who was sobbing. He would give them a couple of moments, his sister-in-law and his brother, and the new life they had created.

Then he had things to do, the umbilical cord, the placenta, the messiness of birth. Things the parents would never remember while they held their baby girl with so much love in their hearts.

When the midwife arrived, running through the front door, there was very little for her to do. But Aaron had never been so pleased to see someone in his entire life.

"YOU DID GOOD," Saul said and cupped his shoulder. He'd moved outside, letting the midwife take over, run checks, and pronounce mom and baby fine. Grace was outside with them, sitting on the small wall around Eddie and Jenny's backyard. She was pale, a hand over her belly, protectively cupping the new life inside her, and Saul moved to sit next to her, bumping shoulders.

"Okay?" he asked.

She looked up at him, startled, and then fled. Not just left but actually sprinted out of the garden and through the side gate to the road. She only lived a block away, but Aaron wondered if he should go after her.

"She'll be fine," Saul said, but he sounded sad.

Aaron didn't have time to question his brother's statement or tone because Eddie appeared at the door, shell-shocked but grinning as wide as the Cheshire Cat.

"Oh my god," he announced, completely spaced out "She's beautiful. Jenny, the baby. They're beautiful." He held up his car keys. "I need to fetch Milly and Jake."

Eddie was in no fit state to drive. Aaron opened his mouth to say he'd do it, but Saul beat him to it, taking the keys, giving Eddie a hard hug, and then using the side gate to head for the car.

Eddie sat next to Aaron and put an arm over his shoulder. "Thank you, little brother."

Aaron huffed a laugh. "I didn't do anything. That was all Jenny."

"And it was all my fault, you know. I looked it up on Google, and it said sex was okay, and she wanted—"

"Stop, okay, I don't want to picture you and Jenny... y'know."

They sat there for a while. Eddie humming under his breath.

"Aaroni, Ariana, Arienne? Aria?" Eddie eased away from Aaron and lifted his face to the sky. "How about Aaroni?"

"What?"

"The baby should be named for you. After all, you delivered her. How about Aaroni? Should we add an S to that? Aaronis? Would that be a silent S? How about Aaronisabelle?"

"No, jeez, poor kid."

"Well, you choose a name then."

"No, asshole, I'm not responsible for her name." They fell into silence, and then an idea formed in Aaron's mind. "Okay, well, how about Mom's name, how about Elizabeth?"

Emotion gripped him. Their mom was long gone, just a distant memory now, but yeah, that seemed like a good idea. He side-hugged Eddie.

"That sounds like a good idea," Eddie said and stood, brushing the brick dust from the wall off his pants. "Elizabeth *Aaronisabelle* Carter."

Aaron smiled and then realized what he'd heard.

"No!" he shouted after Eddie.

"Just kidding, man," Eddie responded and then chuckled evilly as he went into the house.

Chapter Ten
_____

THE LAST TIME ROB HAD BEEN ON A HORSE HE'D BEEN A KID. Maybe seven or eight, if he recalled right. That time had been a disaster as well, the saddle not tight enough, slipping sideways as he tumbled to the ground. That incident had pushed all thoughts of a rodeo career out of his mind, and he'd gotten to this age without feeling the need to go riding again.

Still, the kids wanted to learn, and for some horrific reason, Nate, the big former rodeo star, had said that the best way for the kids to learn was for the grown-ups to show there was nothing to be scared of.

And he wasn't scared. Not exactly. There wasn't much in his life that scared him; not even the bullet fragments that were stealing his life. Or at least, he had a very strong mental trap to hide the fear in, and it only opened on odd occasions.

He just didn't know if riding was a good thing. Hell, it probably wasn't on the list of approved activities when the surgeon said rest would be good. But he wanted the kids to feel he was joining in.

Why did he want that when it went against everything he was aiming for he? Hell if he knew.

I want them to smile, is all.

Nate did all the checks, proficiently, tidily, spoke with great confidence of how the horse was a smooth ride and how the kids would be fine on the smaller ponies when it was their turn.

"Take her around the ring," Nate said and waited. When it dawned on him that Nate wanted him to make the horse *go*, he pressed with his heels, and Dragon moved forward.

And who the hell named a white horse Dragon, and why did it make Rob think that things were going to go to shit?

Which, of course, they did.

Not because of the horse. Dragon was a pussycat who placidly walked around the ring, returning to Nate and accepting a treat for managing not to throw the idiot on its back.

No, the shit was that standing next to the kids, with his niece and nephew, was Aaron. Not only that, but Aaron was smirking. He was probably the best rider in the whole damn world or something.

"Looking good up there, Navy," he said and smirked. The fucker.

"Okay, are we ready?" Nate asked, thankfully interrupting the fact that all Rob wanted to do was get off the horse and rub Aaron's face in the dirt.

Even with an audience.

Out on the trail, with him following Bran and Toby, he managed to avoid talking to Aaron at all, focusing on the fact that his nephews seemed to have some skills with horses. Even the tiny ones they were on. Toby had an assistant, a young girl called Clair, who led his pony and reassured him, but Bran seemed happy to plod along and stay up by gripping everything super tight. Poor pony.

He ignored that Aaron and his two had gotten far ahead now, right up to the lake probably, which was where they were heading. He looked as if being in the saddle was second nature and Rob had a lot of jokes about the state of Aaron's ass if they ever had alone time again.

Which we're not.

When he, Bran, and Toby reached the lake, Nate instructed them on how to tie the ponies off, then settled down with the four kids to talk horse care and all kinds of other things, Clair sitting with them.

Which, of course, left Rob with Aaron, who was stripping out of his clothes.

"Swim?" Aaron asked, standing in swim trunks that clung to muscular thighs and made Rob's imagination go wild.

"That was the idea," Rob said, stripping down to his shorts as well. They had a thirty-minute horse care break, and it seemed as if he had the same idea as Aaron, the lake calling to him.

Now, in the water, that was *his* strength, and as soon as he was away from shore, he headed to the other side of the lake with vigorous movements. He only got halfway before his arms failed to propel him anymore, but he was twenty feet in front of Aaron who reached him, stopped, and trod water.

"How long were you a SEAL?" Aaron asked in the middle of the enormous lake where no one would be able to hear him.

"I wasn't—"

Aaron snorted. "You said you were navy, but you're a heroic idiot. You're clearly in pain, yet you went off like a torpedo from shore, most of that underwater, so tell me, how long were you a SEAL?"

"Long enough," Rob hedged. Discussions about his career would lead to the gaps which would end up with loads of questions he couldn't answer. He'd left his SEAL team when the politics got in the way of being allowed to go into a country and help civilians. And when taking the bad guys out of the equation meant that some higher up in a foreign government was offended.

He'd been ripe picking for Saunders, who recruited him for a new *private* team, along with a quiet kid he'd learned was Justin, and another man, Webb. Saunders and Webb were dead, Justin had seen to that, and everyone above them? They were dead and it was all Rob's doing.

He and Justin were the last ones left standing.

As it should be.

He startled when Aaron touched him, running hands over his shoulders. "You are so tight," he said, and it wasn't a euphemism; it was a medical analysis. "Have you tried acupuncture?" Rob shrugged away, and the movement of water separated them by a few feet.

"We should go back," he said and turned to face the shore, abruptly aware of how far he'd come out, and how fucked his spine was, and how unlikely it would be he'd make it back without suffering for his stupidity.

He'd only struck out like that because he'd wanted to show Aaron that, even though he was shit on horseback, he could swim like an Olympian.

If the Olympian had a mess of scar tissue under his skin on muscles holding him upright.

They made it back to shore at a slower pace, and Aaron stayed with him, the asshole, with his caring and his annoying way of constantly asking if Rob was okay.

"I can help you out," Aaron offered.

"Fuck off," Rob muttered under his breath.

"Idiot Frogman," Aaron replied and then smirked, which gave Rob the push he needed to get out of the water by himself. What really burned was that part of him wanted to lean on Aaron because somehow they had a connection.

Even if Rob had tried to avoid it.

He used the towel he'd thought to bring with him and pulled on jeans.

"Uncle Rob, look!" Toby left the circle of people and trotted over, a notebook in his hand and a wide grin on his face. "I did this for you!"

Tongue poking out, he concentrated on tearing a page from the book and thrust it at his uncle. Rob wiped his hands on his jeans and took the page, turning it to see a stylized black line drawing of a horse, that had been colored in with a surprising amount of purple and green.

"Do you like it?" Toby asked, worrying at a loose tooth with his tongue and looking concerned.

"I love it. We should put it on the fridge when we get back."

"Or when we get a real house," Bran said from behind them.

Rob stiffened. This wasn't the first time Bran had mentioned a real house, but it was the first when he'd let little Toby hear. What did Rob do? Agree, which would give Bran hope, or tell them explicitly that a real home would be somewhere where *he* wasn't?

"That would be great." He took the coward's way out. "Can you look after it? I'm still a bit wet."

Toby nodded and pushed the picture back into the notebook, very carefully, as if it was the most precious of things.

And all Rob could think was that despite what his plans were and how long he had left, the picture was precious.

Sadness pushed its soul-stealing way into his heart, and he couldn't help himself. Something inside him snapped, and he reached for Toby and hugged him.

He wanted to give Toby that one memory of the day at the lake when he'd handed his uncle a picture and gotten a hug in return.

Chapter Eleven

ROB DECIDED THAT EVERYTHING HAD GONE TO SHIT, ALL because it was raining. He didn't know why he was blaming the rain, but because of it, all of Rob's well-laid plans had begun to spiral out of control. So far, he'd introduced the kids around, got them horse riding, making sure they spent time with Sam, even helping Ashley make cakes.

He just wished he could pin Justin down, but he kept disappearing the minute Rob got near him.

And now it was raining, and he'd already read four books to Toby who kept climbing onto his lap. He did a lot of that, clinging to Rob, hugging his leg, asking him to read stories. Rob couldn't help feeling a growing affection for his nephews. After all, they *were* family. He saw his sister in them, but also himself in Bran. With all his bravado and the walls he created to protect him and his brother from the world, he was just like Rob.

They were stuck indoors, the three of them, Bran and Toby at the window looking out at the heavy downpour and whispering.

"Mom used to take us out in the rain," Bran said and turned away from the window to face Rob.

Rob remembered his sister loving the rain, almost as much as Rob loved to swim. How had he forgotten that? His memories of Suzi had been pushed down for so long, and he missed her. A weight settled in his heart. He'd never got to say goodbye to her, but all that time he was away she'd still loved him, still thought of him.

Hell, she'd given her family to him.

"I wanna go out," Toby announced.

Toby had become so much more confident around Rob, and he couldn't decide if that was a good thing or not. The little hellion loved to climb all over him, pretending he was a tree or something, and poked at Rob every chance he could.

He liked the curious little boy who was learning his new world so fast.

No, it was more than like. It was love. Rob wanted to be there for him in a way that was hopeless to imagine.

And how had that happened? Since when was feeling sorry for himself an option?

"We don't have coats," he said. He had to be the sensible one, right?

Bran shoved open the window and held out his hand, his nose wrinkled in concentration. "It's warm rain," he decreed, which was enough to have Toby scrambling down and pulling on the tiny boots that Gabe had dropped off for them both yesterday.

"Let's go!" he said and bounced on his toes.

Rob guessed it wouldn't hurt to go for a quick walk. It was nearly lunchtime, and they all needed to eat.

"To Branches," he announced, opened the door, and led the two boys out. Which didn't last for long when they scampered ahead and danced in the rain. There was yelling and laughing and jumping in puddles, and Rob tried his damnedest not to find it heartwarming in any way. He loved that the boys played together, wished nothing more for them than that they could live their lives normally and close to each other, as part of a caring community.

They reached the bridge, and the boys went up on tiptoes, looking over the side as best they could, which wasn't all that well. Then something happened. Rob was close but couldn't hear them, and under the canopy of the tree by the bridge, he saw that Toby was crying.

Bran pulled Toby into his arms and held him, and he was sobbing so hard. Rob moved closer, not sure what to do.

"I miss Mom," Toby said, and Bran rocked him.

Part of the shell around Rob's heart splintered. Would it mess up his plans to comfort them? It wasn't as if casual affection meant anything to them at all. He could be the grown-up here, the kindly uncle they needed until he moved on. He went straight to his knees and held out his hands, and for a second he thought they wouldn't move until suddenly he had his arms full of two children who clung to him as if, somehow, he could make things right.

I don't have time to make things right for anyone.

He held them close, and they talked about Suzi, about how she had long hair, and baked cookies, and how she'd been ill.

What he was doing was helping. He had to be sure of it. The world moved on as they talked. People walked by, but no one stopped to ask what was wrong, even though they were sitting under the tree in the rain on the wet ground. Why would they ask? The three of them had their backs to the bridge and were chatting quietly after Toby had stopped crying, and everyone was too polite to call them out on any of that.

"She loved Bunny as much as I do," Toby offered as his last comment on the matter. "I 'member that."

How many memories of their mom would they have after he left? The only one who could tell them about her childhood was him. He pulled up the first thing he could recall, one of his earliest memories.

"Your mom had a teddy. She called him Freddy and carried it everywhere when she was little. But the stuffing fell out because she loved him so much, and I had to fix him. All we had were staples, and she carried him around for a long time after." He remembered Freddy was on her bed the night he'd left, at eighteen, for the navy. The last time he'd seen her.

Silence.

"Freddie was in the box with her," Bran said in a hushed whisper.

That didn't make sense to Rob until horribly, it did. His sister, their mom, had been buried with the teddy? Grief flooded him, the kind of grief he had to stop feeling. He didn't have time for it, and each day they were there, without him settling everything for the kids, was another day of his life gone.

He stood up and brushed himself off.

"Come on, kids, lunch."

By the time they made it to Branches, sitting at a table in the corner, both of them had calmed down and seemed to want to talk about their mom, and all Rob could do was listen, even as he was hoping that Sam would make an appearance. It was his place after all. But it seemed other people were working the restaurant right now, and that didn't bode well for the kids getting the chance to connect with Sam and Justin. Maybe he needed to put more of his focus on

Ashley and Gabe. Yes, they were having a new baby, but that wasn't such an obstacle, right?

"Mom always said you were lost when you were away being a hero, Uncle Rob," Bran said, pulling him from his thoughts, "and that was why you couldn't come and get us. She was sad about it sometimes."

The arrival of their salads interrupted the flow of questions, but Bran was nothing if not tenacious.

"So what kind of hero were you?" he persisted and concentrated on piling lettuce on his fork.

"Were you a soldier?" Toby asked. Possibly the first real direct question he'd ever given Rob.

"Kind of," Rob answered vaguely, "but not a hero, just someone doing a job."

"Yeah, she said that as well. But you must have known about us, right? About Toby and me?"

Both of them stared at him, waiting for an explanation. How did he explain that he'd tried not to know a thing, that apart from the fact they'd been born, he hadn't wanted to form any bond with them or with his sister?

The sacrifice was big.

The sacrifice was the only way to keep them, and everyone else in this country, safe.

"I was away a lot," he finally offered. The sad part of that was that neither of them seemed to question the statement.

By the time they'd seen the horses and made it back to the cabin, his back ached like a bitch, and the tingling in his left arm wouldn't stop. The docs had warned him about this, poison from the bullet leaching into his body, giving him a rough idea of when he'd have no choices left. He tried not to think about it, but when the day was done, the kids safely in bed, and everywhere locked up, he gave in and took the Fentanyl.

The relief was almost instant. The experts told him that with his limited timeframe and as the end drew near, he wouldn't be able to live without the painkillers. He'd proved them wrong for much of the time; he'd managed without them for a while now. In the days they'd been at Crooked Tree, this was only the second time he'd given in.

The pain was not taking him down, not after everything else he'd survived.

Sleep was a long time coming, but at least it wasn't the pain that kept him awake, but instead the nagging guilt that he should have been there for Suzi. He could have held her hand when she'd found out she had cancer, supported her even as she was dying, maybe looked after his nephews.

But he hadn't. He'd put his country before his own family, and now he was paying for it.

You made your choice. Live with it, asshole.

Something woke Rob. A noise, a whispered call of his name, he wasn't sure. All he knew was that when he opened his eyes again, it was dark and someone was sitting on the end of his bed. This second visit to him when he was sleeping was getting old.

Justin held up the box of Fentanyl, tossing it in his hand and catching it deftly.

"Want to tell me what this is for?"

"What the fuck are you doing in here again? I thought you'd be past this stalking me in my sleep by now."

Justin ignored him. "And I say again. Why the heavy meds?"

Rob was sure he'd put them away in his bedside cabinet, so Justin had gotten in and rummaged through his drawer, all while he slept. Not to mention the small bedside lamp was on, although Rob couldn't exactly remember if he'd left it on. Sleeping with a light on had become his new normal in case the pain got to be too much, and he couldn't see the way to the bathroom to be sick.

Getting sloppy now.

"I was injured; I'm in pain." He sat up, refusing to show any of the aches he was feeling from a combination of the injury he was hiding.

Justin kept tossing that damn box and regarded him thoughtfully. "You remember the Clemens job; the arms deals out of Boston?"

"Justin—"

"You remember the bullet you took, high up in the thigh? It didn't have an exit wound, and you walked on that leg for six, maybe seven hours, and you wouldn't even take one solitary Tylenol."

"I didn't need meds, I had adrenaline."

"You forget I know you, Rob. I *know* you are as stubborn as fuck and you refuse to allow yourself a single moment of vulnerability. You've got ice for blood and a heart too hard to be pretend-daddy to two kids. So you want to start that again? Oh, and while you're at it, tell me what the fuck you are *really* doing here."

Rob twisted on the bed, placing his feet on the floor. He didn't want to be stuck under sheets if he had a former special agent in his room. Rob Brady didn't show weakness to anyone, least of all one as highly trained as Justin.

"I told you that as well. I'm visiting my only friend."

Justin tossed the box in the air again, and looked at him thoughtfully. "What. Are. You. Doing. Here?" he asked and stood, stepping closer, so there was only a foot between them.

"I don't have any fucking idea!" He shouted, because he couldn't keep the tension stuffed inside him anymore. "I'm desperate and I have nowhere else to go."

Justin stared at him, and waited. The asshole wasn't letting this alone.

"All I know is I'm a dad now, you know," Rob began because that seemed like the simplest place to start. "Not exactly a dad in the strictest biological sense of being a father, but I'm all that Bran and Toby have." Being an uncle wasn't news. He'd been one since Bran was born eight years ago, followed a few years later by Toby. He just hadn't seen his nephews up close, and they existed in a nebulous world he never thought he'd see. Until a fucking bullet tore into him.

"And?" Justin prompted him, and Rob realized he'd slipped into another train of thought and that his brain was fuzzy from the meds.

"Can we...?" he glanced at his watch, the luminous dial displaying 3:10 a.m. "I need coffee."

Justin blocked him from leaving. "Don't change the fucking subject, asshole."

It was all Rob could do not to curl up back on the bed and will Justin to leave, but he needed to clear his damn head and talk honestly. So he confronted the naked aggression in Justin and held his ground.

"I need coffee, and then I'll talk."

Justin let him pass, followed him close, refused a coffee, and then it was a matter of where to open up and maybe get the shit kicked out of him. Certainly not in the cabin. Might as well use the trees as he'd done with Aaron. He led Justin away from the cabin to the trees. Finding the tree stump and sitting on it, all while trying not to wince. Where did he start? With picking up the kids? Or getting shot? Or even further back?

"My sister died, and I wasn't there. I wasn't anywhere, actually. They couldn't find me."

Justin took the trunk opposite him, although he looked as

if he wanted to be anywhere but sitting there. Or maybe it was just that he was wary of the truth. Compassion spiked in Rob. Did Justin think this was something to do with him?

Of course, he does. You turned up in the middle of the night, and you haven't left yet.

"No one was supposed to find either of us," Justin murmured. "That was the whole point."

"But she was dying."

"My dad had cancer, and I couldn't be there for him. It was hard but it was who we were."

"At least you checked in on them. I never checked on Suzi or the kids. I cut myself out of their lives as if I were dead."

"So? Nothing you ever said to me made me think you wanted to be around family, or hell, that you even had a family. So why the crap about feelings now?"

"I broke cover because I needed to say goodbye."

How did he even begin to explain how he'd had to change? What was it about that small weight of metal wedged against his spine that had rendered him a sap who thought he should reconnect to family before he ended his life? Should he even tell Justin what he was doing? That he was planning to leave the kids and vanish again, and that he'd drawn up a will assigning guardianship of the kids to Justin, along with the phone number of the governor who had aided him? What would Justin think? Perhaps it was just best to start from the beginning.

"Goodbye to your sister."

"And the kids."

Justin looked thoughtful. "You mean in case something happened?"

Rob shook his head. "Not in case. Because something *did* happen. I always thought I'd die on the job, you know. We were good agents, but it was inevitable that one day even *you* would be forced to turn against me the same way I was sent to kill you. Right?"

Justin was expressionless. When Rob had visited him last, Justin had asked that Rob kill him away from others, where he wouldn't be found. He'd never questioned that Rob would kill him at all. It was just accepted.

"Well, I'm not killing you, so cut to the chase, Rob," he growled.

"A bullet nearly took me out. A few millimeters either way, and I would have bled out, job done, lying underneath the mark I'd agreed to dispatch. He was a particularly evil motherfucker."

"You were shot. Okay, it hurts, probably like a bitch, which explains the Fentanyl."

Rob realized he was skipping to the end of this story, and he had much more that he needed Justin to understand. He closed his eyes briefly and then started even further back.

"My parents passed away five years ago, Dad to early-onset Alzheimer's, Mom to pneumonia six months later. I didn't go to their funerals. Other things were more important. Saving lives, keeping the country safe. You know how it was."

"What the hell does that have to do with the meds? I don't need a history lesson on the Brady family."

Justin leaned back against the curve of a tree beside the old stump, as if he was there for the night, and for a moment, Rob directly stared at his friend. Justin looked good, less haunted, happy, his eyes clear of the awful shadows of guilt. But under the peace, he knew Justin was still that man who'd stood next to Rob and cleared the country of homegrown terrorists. Justin had been a hard, blunt tool, and that much was still inside him.

"My sister died, but I didn't know. It happened about the same time I was injured, a year back, but she was gone."

"Side question here. What the hell were you doing on a job anyway? You told me you were done."

Trust Justin to focus on that. "I was talking about my sister."

"We'll get to that, meanwhile, what kind of authorization did you have to be on this *job*, Rob?"

"Classified."

Justin cursed loudly. "You said you were out."

"From the team, yes, but that didn't mean the bad guys gave up trying to kill people out there. I freelanced."

"God, Rob, you had the chance to retire, to make something real for the rest of your life."

Rob ignored the concern in his friend's unspoken *same as me*, and forged ahead. "So I was making things right, you know, and I turned up at the address I had."

"To say goodbye to her, because she was dying."

"No. Yes."

"Which is it?"

"Look, I didn't even know she was ill, and I get there and find she's died, and my nephews are in the care of Child Services, and I'm their only living relative. It was all there in black and white. I'm all they have. I should have jumped at the chance at having them with me."

Justin tensed as if Rob's intentions hit him squarely. "What do you mean 'should'?"

"I was going to leave them where they were." Rob closed his eyes momentarily. He shouldn't forget that Justin knew him well, understood that he was hard and a loner.

"What the hell? They're your blood."

"We didn't all have lives like you had, J," he snapped and then sighed noisily. "Jesus, yes, for the first week, all I could think was what was the point in me having them? Two kids so young. They'd lost their mom, and abruptly they have an asshole uncle as temporary guardian?"

"So what changed?"

"I researched the family they were with, and I didn't like the dad. Bran said he'd never hurt them, but I didn't like him." He rubbed his chest. "I didn't like what I saw, so I needed to make sure they had a place I was happy with."

He didn't give much away, but Justin would read between the lines anyway.

"Not with you," he said.

Rob nodded. "No."

"But you *clearly* changed your mind because they're with you now?"

"No."

Justin frowned, and he didn't seem so relaxed. "What are you doing here at Crooked Tree then?" Even as he asked the question, his expression changed from confusion to temper. Apparently, the penny had dropped, and he'd come to the right conclusion all on his own.

"Justin—"

"What the fuck, Rob! Were you leaving them here? What? With me? Jesus, what the hell—?"

"Let me explain."

By now Justin was standing, looming over him, his expression incredulous, and his hands in fists at his sides. Rob stood as well, pain knifing down his legs, and they faced off like they had done so many times before.

But this wasn't a level playing field; Rob was desperate.

Justin's expression was hard. "If you don't want your own flesh and blood, then surely there is another foster family?"

And that was the question that plagued him. There must be good families out there, but who would make sure the foster family looked after the kids when he was gone? At least here at Crooked Tree, he knew that Justin would watch out for them.

He held up a hand to get Justin to back away, and after a moment he did at least take a step back, although he was bristling with temper.

"I was sitting in a room after I'd done the research. It was papered with posters about foster care, about how special people were needed for exceptional children. Just as Bran sitting opposite me frowning and accusing me all at the same time. Or Toby who was sniffling into the sleeve of his jacket and hiccupping a sob every so often. What could I say when Child Services said I had permission to take them?"

"I'm so confused right now," Justin said carefully.

It was now or never.

"Fuck, Justin, I'm dying," Rob announced. "I had to say goodbye because I only had three months to live."

At first, it seemed as if Justin hadn't heard him. He blinked at Rob and said nothing, and then he shoved at him.

"Don't lie to me, Rob."

Rob sat, the shooting pain in his left leg making him feel wobbly and nauseous. He'd come to terms with dying when he'd been told, not really wishing for anything in his life in particular, but now he needed to call on that nebulous friendship he had with Justin to ask for help.

"I swear I'm not lying. The bullet, or what was left of it, is lodged near my spine. Too near to remove it safely, and it's encased in scar tissue, leaching lead into my bloodstream, causing mild paralysis in my limbs and a shit-ton of pain from the mess in my muscles. Oh, and memory loss which is fucking shitty."

Justin stared at him, so many emotions flickering over his

face that Rob couldn't make them all out. He was looking for the lie, trying to see if he could trust Rob.

"Christ," Justin said and slumped back onto his seat.

"I was told the kind of life I might have after an operation, and I don't mean the outcome where I die on the table, but the other one where I am paralyzed and a burden to everyone and no one because I don't have anyone. So, I'm here, with whatever time I have left, dosed up on Fentanyl, finding somewhere safe for my family and asking my *friend* to help me."

Justin closed his eyes. The glow from the cabin highlighted the tension in his expression. Then his eyes snapped open. "Wait. What did you say?"

"I'm asking a friend—"

"No, you said there *was* something they could do? An operation with specific outcomes." Justin prompted.

A small part of Rob died inside. He didn't want Justin believing there was a way out of this.

"No."

"Rob—"

"Paralyzed, Justin. Or dead. Okay? The bullet's so high it would be from the neck down, and then what would I be to those boys? Nothing. I'm taking what time I have left and making my life count for a change, going out fighting. For Bran and Toby. Finding them a family. You get that, right?"

Justin scrubbed at his eyes with the heel of his hands. "Make your life count? What we did, saving lives, that means we already count, asshole."

"Not in the same way, not to me. When my sister was here, when she had her family, that was what I was fighting for, okay? It gave me purpose, a reason for what we were doing. I thought I was working for my country, but when it came down to it, I think I was fighting for my nephews, for their future. I'm still fighting for them now."

"But you've just told me you're happy to walk away from them?"

"Justin, are you even listening to me? I'm not deciding to leave. I have no choice at all. I have maybe another two months left now before the pain is too much, and I want this done before I take myself off somewhere to end my life." *I need this to be done.* "You can take all the money I have. I need you to promise me you will look after the boys, keep them here."

"I don't need your money." Justin sounded tired.

"But you'll look out for the boys for me? They could have family here, be a part of your life. Sam would feed them all the best stuff, and you could teach them to ride, and tell them that their uncle Rob did love them in his own way."

Justin went quiet; his head bowed, his fingers laced together. Then he glanced up.

"What happens to you? Hmm? Will the bullet end up killing you on its own? Or do you mean you're taking your own life, somehow?"

"Maybe the bullet will get there first, but soon the pain will be too much, and yeah, I'm going to take myself out of the equation."

He waited for Justin to call him a coward, but knew he'd never say that.

"Selfish fucker," Justin murmured.

Rob tensed, but he'd already run through the thoughts about what he was doing being selfish. But he'd always ended up knowing he was doing the right thing.

"I know you can't talk for Sam," Rob murmured. "But, please, Justin, consider doing this for Bran and Toby."

"No."

Rob's heart sank. He'd been pinning everything on Justin. "Please, Justin."

"I didn't mean no, to Bran and Toby. I meant, no, I can't talk for Sam." He shook his head as he spoke, and Rob's chest tightened.

"I understand," he said, even though hope was slowly slipping away.

"But I know Sam, and his heart is big enough for more than just me." He regarded Rob steadily. "You think we would throw them out? As long as Bran and Toby need a home, they'll have one at Crooked Tree. Maybe not with Sam and me, who knows, but they will have family."

Relief flooded Rob, and he rose to his feet at the same time as Justin, his hand outstretched, waiting to shake on the offer. Justin ignored his hand, pulling him in for a hug instead.

"I'm sorry for you and your selfish, stupid decision, but mostly I'm sorry for them because they won't get to know you thoroughly," Justin said. Then conversation over, he left.

ROB MANAGED to get back to bed, although he didn't sleep at first, despite the remnants of Fentanyl in his system. He could go now and be at peace. Somehow, sleep pulled him under, and he woke to the light weight of the boys sitting on his sheets. They appeared uncertain, and he knew he should send them back to their bedroom, be the hard-hearted asshole they couldn't love. Make them not want him but want Sam and Justin instead.

Instead, he opened his arms, and they crawled into his hold, and he inhaled the scent of them as they snuggled in.

"We had dreams," Bran murmured.

"With monsters," Toby added, Bunny squashed between them.

"There's no such thing as monsters," Rob said and moved right to the edge of the bed in case they thought he was comforting them.

Pity he was lying. There were monsters out there. Real people with guns and bombs who wanted to kill and maim. That was the kind of terrors that formed his nightmares.

When he woke the next time, the boys were standing at the end of his bed.

"We had breakfast, and Toby wants to learn to swim," Bran informed him. "I could show him, but I need help."

"Let's go." Toby bounced on his toes.

Wait, this wasn't right. They needed to distance themselves from him. He should call Justin and ask him to take them.

"No," he said and hid his face under the sheet, torn between wanting to show them and continuing to build the wall to protect them from his disappearance.

He peeked out to see them both still there and Toby still bouncing.

"Uncle Rob needs coffee," Bran said and then vanished into the kitchen, Toby going with him.

Rob rolled up out of bed, breathing through the pain and dressing in shorts and a T-shirt. Then he padded in to find coffee, taking over from Bran who had managed to spill beans and was confused by the buttons on the machine. At least the delay gave the low-grade meds he'd taken time to work, and by the time they'd started walking up the hill, he felt halfway human.

The first swimming lesson was a compromise of sorts because they didn't go up to Silver Lake, instead heading for a small pond outside the Todd place. There were deeper parts to the water there, but he wanted to see exactly how much confidence they had before he took them to the big glacial Silver Lake.

If I'm still here. I can leave now that Justin said he'd have my back...

They started with bobbing around, with their feet on the bottom, and Bran showed that he was actually a good swimmer and was happy to go a little farther each time as long as Rob stayed with Toby, who was anxious. In the end, Rob floated on his back with both boys clinging to him, chattering on and on about everything and nothing, and practicing treading water. Neither boy panicked, and Rob was proud of them both.

"He's gonna be a good swimmer," Bran confided as Toby took a few hesitant strokes away from Rob's grasp before doggy paddling back to him, grinning widely. The scared, quiet little boy was disappearing before his eyes, replaced by a kid who really wanted to spread his wings.

"So can we go to Silver Lake now?" Bran asked as they walked back to the cabin.

"Maybe another day."

"Okay, maybe on Sunday when Milly and Jake come here."

Toby walked next to his brother, but they weren't holding hands.

Having to stay here three more days, maybe teaching Toby and Bran to swim, giving them a happy memory of the kind of person that Rob was? Swimming with the children, *and* seeing Aaron?

Maybe I will stay just a few more days.

IT TURNED out he didn't have to wait until Sunday to see Aaron.

He visited again that night, late because his shift had just ended, and wordlessly led Rob to the trees. The quick mindless sex was just what he needed, right up against that same tree. This time it was him bracing against the aged wood. Aaron held him as if he weighed nothing, forced him to feel every breathtaking moment of his orgasm, collapsing against him briefly and then stepping back.

"This is getting to be a habit," Aaron murmured.

Rob turned to face him. "Twice is not a habit."

Aaron buttoned himself up and winked. "It will be after the next time."

"There isn't going to be a next time," Rob snapped and leaned more on the tree.

"That's what you say. See you next time."

With a flash of that familiar sexy smile, Aaron vanished into the dark. Rob wanted to slide bonelessly down the tree, but if he did that, he might never get back up again. He managed to hobble inside, locked up, showered, grabbed water and his meds. Swallowing the Fentanyl, he then staggered to bed, knowing he would pay for what he'd just done in the morning.

But was sure he'd agree to do it all again.

WHICH THEY DID.

Two nights in a row.

And fuck, it was becoming more than a habit because he wanted it each time Aaron appeared.

Chapter Twelve

When Aaron woke up late on Sunday, his first thought was of Rob. Not breakfast, work, going for a run, or what was happening in the news. Nope. His first thoughts were all about Rob.

The kissing was hot.

The press of him too perfect.

And that was dangerous. There were too many messy feelings caught up in their casual hookups, and he didn't know what to make of them. Also, he couldn't act on the hot, insistent need to visit the enigmatic man, because Saul would kill him if he didn't turn up for the family dinner. Saul didn't ask for much, but he'd been quiet ever since Michaela had died, so it was an easy decision to make. Anyway, it was little Elizabeth's first official family dinner, and family always came first.

Still, last night had been the fourth hookup, and each time was better. The first time had been getting off with no idea what Rob liked, but last night had been intense. Aaron had taken control of it all and had held Rob on the edge for so long he'd sagged against Aaron when he'd finished. There was a power in that, in being able to take a man like Rob and make him feel everything.

They'd actually talked a little. Words that weren't sarcastic or aimed at creating the most hurt. Of course, it had been little more than him asking Rob about the kids, and Rob replying they were fine and could Aaron get the fuck on with sucking his cock.

But, yeah, words.

He headed out to Carters really early when he'd run out of things to do at home, feeling lighter knowing he'd see everyone, but knowing he wouldn't be saying anything about Rob. He imagined explaining that he was intrigued by a secretive man who refused to give him any emotional connection. That would go down well. They'd all give him advice about how to talk Rob into a real bed and how Aaron should really grow up already and get a relationship that involved more than sex. They would talk about how Elijah had been gone a long time now and that Aaron needed to move on. Then they would agree collectively that Elijah had been a good man and that it must have hurt for Aaron to lose him.

So, not telling the family was a good thing.

"What the hell are you doing here already?" Saul asked immediately. "Go away and come back when it's time."

"No way. I'm here to see my big brother." He knew he was two hours early, but that usually didn't matter. In fact, some of the best conversations he'd had with Saul were when they were alone prepping Sunday dinner. Or rather, Saul prepped, and he hung around drinking coffee.

"Please just go," Saul said, and Aaron got a good look at his brother's face, at the exhaustion marking his eyes, and the pain in his expression.

"What's wrong?" Aaron asked immediately.

Saul glanced at the door to his apartment, and Aaron knew that expression, the one that said Saul had a *friend* upstairs in his apartment. That was good news. Saul didn't take enough time for himself. Although with the way Saul was smacking steak around, it didn't seem as if he'd worked off his stress with hot, sweaty sex.

"Who is it?" Aaron asked and sneaked a carrot from a pile. "Whoever it is, she should stay for dinner."

Saul cursed under his breath but didn't repeat it loud enough for Aaron to hear.

"Seriously, we all know you're seeing someone. You should ask her to stay. Tell her we'll be nice and that we won't argue too much, and we'll even keep the kids quiet, and tell her—"

"I ask her every Sunday to come here, okay? She always says no," Saul snapped and rapped the back of Aaron's hand with a spoon.

"Ow, what was that for?"

"I weighed those fucking carrots," he snapped and pulled another one out of the pantry, placing it with the pile and chopping it with a knife so sharp that Aaron was concerned it would take a finger off. "Just leave, please."

"What crawled up your ass and died?"

Saul ignored him, so Aaron pressed ahead with the questions about the mystery lady.

"Why doesn't she stay, then?"

"Seriously, you need to leave," Saul said and opened the back door, pointing out to the yard. "Come back in an hour."

Aaron stood his ground. Something wasn't right here. Saul was defeated as if the weight of the world wasn't just on his shoulders, but was pressing the life out of him.

"What's wrong?" he asked and hooked a stool to sit at the counter.

"Nothing," Saul lied and decimated a head of broccoli, shoving it to one side, then bracing his arms on the counter. He side-eyed Aaron. "Everything."

Saul's apartment's internal door opened, and he looked over, ready to be on his best behavior for whomever Saul was seeing. Only it was Grace who walked in from Saul's room. Not in the EMT uniform he was used to seeing her in, but in soft jeans and a cornflower-blue shirt with tears streaking her face.

Aaron's first instinct was that Grace was here to see him, some work thing maybe, but then it hit him that she'd walked out of Saul's private apartment, that there was no reason for her to be here today and she was certainly not to see him. So, was this Saul's mystery woman?

"Grace? Did you…? Wait, you and Saul…?"

She tilted her chin. "We're not talking about this, Aaron."

It was one of *those* conversations when more was said with body language than actual words. She had her arms crossed over her chest, daring him to say a damn thing. Sue him, but he needed to get an idea as to what the hell was happening here.

"You and Saul," he repeated.

"What?" she shouted. "You have a problem with that, too? Want to make some comment about how your big brother is too old for me, that he's going to be seventy when my baby is in college? Or maybe that you think he's right when he says I need to find someone closer to my age? Well, look how well that worked out for him and me." She pressed a hand to her belly, and tears started to flow.

Aaron stood, thinking he should pull Grace in for a hug or something. Now the story of the on-off relationship from Saul, and the added bit from Grace about being sent away and having a one-night stand, made sense.

Saul's shoulders sagged, and that one action let Aaron see more than Saul probably wanted him to. It seemed he'd walked into a whole mess of arguments here.

"Saul, wait, are you the father…is the baby…?"

"No," Grace snapped.

"No," Saul said at the same time, his words broken.

"Then…" Aaron was utterly lost for words, but he saw the pain in Saul's eyes and tears in Grace's. "I'm so happy for you two," he finally said because that was the truth of the matter, even if it made Grace cry harder and for devastation to cross Saul's face. "I don't think Saul is too old for you."

"Don't be happy for us," Grace sobbed and dropped her hands to her sides, before pointing at Saul. "Because *he* says we're done."

Saul hung his head, but he didn't make a move to stop her as she left, slamming the door behind her.

For a few moments, there was silence.

"Saul—"

"Don't, okay? It's for the best. We've only been seeing each other again for a few weeks, so it's not like it's going to break her heart."

"Did you not see her face? The tears? What the hell did you say to her?"

Saul sat heavily on the nearest stool. "Shit." He scrubbed his face with his hands and wouldn't meet Aaron's gaze. "I don't know anything anymore."

"You need to go after her."

"No, this way is for the best."

"That sounds like self-sacrificing bullshit, Saul. Jesus, how long have you been seeing Grace?"

"There's nothing selfless about it, and we've been seeing each other on and off for a few years. Mostly off."

Grace never struck him as an on-off person, more like the

kind of woman who was looking for Mr. Right. He tried to recall when he'd seen her with a boyfriend of any kind, and he couldn't think of anything concrete. Was that because she'd been hiding the fact that she'd been seeing his brother? Hell, was it Aaron's fault this was all a secret? Saul was suspiciously quiet. How had Aaron not seen this before?

"Keep talking, Saul."

"We broke up. I sent her away, told her she needed to find someone her own age, and she did, and it was once, and she got pregnant. But that is okay because I'm twenty years older than her. You see that, right? You can see that I'm right about it. The baby will grow up without me. I can't be a dad. The barriers are too big. I'm giving her the chance to be with someone who can grow old with her and not two decades years faster."

Saul had that stubborn expression, the one that his brothers were used to when he fought battles for them. So why wasn't he fighting for Grace now?

The back door slammed open again, and Grace stormed in. Evidently, she'd decided that she wasn't leaving at all and today was the time to have this out.

"You can't do this. You can't send me away! I'm not going without a fight," she shouted, and Aaron was stuck in the kitchen in what seemed like a showdown between his brother and his work partner. There was a lot of shouting, which Aaron tried not to listen to as he edged around them to get out of the other door to the upstairs apartment. It was Ryan's old place and would have a sofa or something.

"I don't want to fight!" Saul said.

"I love you!"

"And I love you."

She subsided, and tears rolled down her face. "I know you can never love the baby, but—"

"What! I love you. I'll love the baby."

"Then why are we even shouting at each other?"

Saul made a broken sound. "I don't know."

But everything abruptly went quiet, the shouting stopped, and Aaron chanced a look at the two of them.

They were smiling uncertainly at each other, and it was so beautiful it made Aaron's chest tighten. He'd seen Saul with women before but never with this much love and affection in his expression.

"Pretend I'm not here," Aaron said. "I've seen nothing."

She flushed even more, and Saul shoved him, going to her side and then both of them going out into the yard. Probably to say goodbye in a proper kissing kind of way.

Saul came back in after a short while and carried on with preparing the meat and said nothing at all.

"So? Don't leave me in suspense. Are we going to talk about what just happened?" Aaron asked when they'd worked in silence for a while, him halfheartedly chopping the remaining carrots, and Saul humming along to a song on the radio.

"Probably not. I mean, she's gone home to get changed and to come back for dinner. And, oh yeah, I asked her to marry me," Saul said evenly.

"Holy shit!" Aaron shouted and pulled his brother in for a hug.

When they were young, when Saul had taken responsibility for his brothers, the youngest, Ryan, had been only one. Saul had become a father overnight. He'd never asked a woman to marry him. This was a big freaking deal.

"You'll make such a good husband and dad," Aaron finally offered.

Saul smiled. "Thank you."

Everyone else arrived, but Grace hadn't come back just

yet, probably to give Saul some time with his family. As soon as everyone was in the kitchen, Saul began to talk.

"I wanted to get some—" Saul started and then stopped. Aaron was tuned into Saul, but the others hadn't heard the soft words. "Can I have some time to say...?"

"Guys!" Aaron said and whistled until everyone stopped talking. "Saul has something to say."

The glare Saul shot him wasn't one of gratitude. Instead, he was wary. Maybe he'd deliberately pitched his voice lower so that no one would listen to him. Well, tough. In this family, the brothers lived and died by the Carter rule of honesty and openness, and Saul was no exception.

"I've been seeing someone. It's Grace, Aaron's partner." He pushed ahead before anyone could say anything. "She's only thirty-four, and as you all know, she's pregnant, but I'm not the dad, and before you ask, that is her story to tell, and I'm fifty-four so I'm twenty years older than her, but I love her, and I asked her to marry me." He paused from saying all of that on one long breath. "So. Yeah. Now you know."

Silence. One brother looking at the next. Ryan serious. Eddie smirking. Jason open-mouthed.

"Hang on a minute," Ryan said. "Grace is only thirty-four? Wow, she looks *much* younger than that."

"Thirty-three at least," Eddie said seriously.

"It doesn't matter, because twenty years is nothing. I once read a story about this hundred-year-old guy who was a new dad." Jason was thoughtful. "That guy from *Star Trek*."

"Scottie, James Doohan, and he was seventy-nine or eighty," Ryan confirmed.

Eddie thumped him on the arm. "You're such a nerd."

Ryan shoved him back.

"Oh my god, even more diapers at Sunday dinner!" Jason faked being horrified.

"You think Grace can put up with Saul's snoring?"

"No one can do that."

"Who will be the best man?" Jason mused. "I guess Eddie is the second eldest, but I would look way better in a suit."

"Not as good as me," Eddie replied.

"We should ask Jordan," Ryan said. "I have one sexy boyfriend who looks hella good in a suit."

Aaron smiled as he listened to his brothers, and saw Saul's expression relax a little. None of what Saul had said worried them or shocked them, and in their own way, they were making things easier for him,

So it was his turn to talk. "What my idiot brothers are trying to say is that we guess you love her, and we're so happy that our family is adding someone else."

Saul nodded. "Yes."

"Yep," Jason agreed. "Grace is cool, and you're the best dad we ever had."

"What he said," Eddie added.

"Me three," Ryan said.

Aaron rested a hand on Saul's. "Me four."

The time it took before a nervous Grace arrived meant dinner was cold before anyone actually ate. The congratulations were loud, the questions many, and Saul announced the best man would have to be chosen by lottery unless everyone shut the hell up right the hell now.

When dinner was finished, Aaron collected up his niece and nephew for their normal horse riding and felt the tug of wanting to see Rob again. In daylight. Face-to-face and not fucking each other up against a tree in the dark. He had one long hour to himself, and seeing Rob? Yep, this sounded good.

He made a big show of being dragged from the house by Milly and Jake, but the anticipation was delicious, and they made it to Crooked Tree in good time. He dropped his niece and nephew with Luke, then hurried down the hill and to Rob's place, only slowing down when he got closer so he didn't appear *too* eager. He sauntered around the back, finding Rob exactly where he'd thought. There was no sign of the kids, but that didn't mean anything.

"Hey."

Rob stood immediately and opened the door into the cabin, but this time he didn't close and lock it. He left it wide open and waited in the shadows.

"Sam took the boys for lunch ten minutes ago. They'll be gone for a while," he said, and that was enough to get Aaron moving. They were in each other's arms as soon as the door closed, the kisses heated. Aaron had his hands in Rob's pants as soon as he could, but he wanted this slow. He wanted more than just a quick fuck and done.

For a second they stared at each other.

Aaron's tongue darted out to dampen his lips, and Rob stared at the action. He closed the distance between them and curled his hand around the back of Aaron's head.

"Don't think for one minute you are controlling what happens here," Aaron stated.

"And you think you are?" Rob said and laughed as he gripped Aaron's neck tighter.

Aaron pushed Rob back, and it was *so* on. They kissed, even as they fought to control the kiss, and Aaron pushed his knee between Rob's spread legs, widening them, then shifting a little, so Rob was pushed up, the weight of his groin on Aaron's thigh. He was pinned, and he couldn't move, couldn't balance himself, and it was Aaron who had all the control.

Chapter Thirteen

ROB COULDN'T REMEMBER THE LAST TIME HE'D LET SOMEONE else make the decisions or orchestrate a hookup. He couldn't recall, but it wasn't as if he was capable of deciding here. He'd got to that place where sensation outweighed thought, and the taste of it was intoxicating

Aaron kissed him and silently demanded that Rob give in to him, and Rob didn't have an argument with that.

"I want you bent over the railing," Aaron said into the kiss. "Do you know how much I want my cock inside you. I want everything."

He went to his knees, holding Rob steady, unbuttoning his jeans, and had his mouth on Rob's cock so quickly that he nearly came right there and then. When Aaron pressed his hands to hard thighs, it was game over. He didn't last long, so turned on and burning that all Aaron had to do was suck him down over and over. He reached to push a hand in Aaron's hair, warning him.

Aaron moved off, twisted his fingers on Rob's cock, and Rob was done. His orgasm explosive and he ignored the pain as he came.

"See what it's like when you give up control?" Aaron said cockily as he stood and kissed his open mouth, licking inside and stealing his breath.

Rob wished he could answer, but all he wanted was to show Aaron what giving up control was like. If only his back would let him.

"Maybe it's me bending you over the railing," Rob snapped.

Aaron laughed and deliberately unbuttoned his jeans, pushing the material down and freeing his hard cock.

"How about you return the blow job? That would be a start."

Rob shoved Aaron then, and he was caught off balance, tumbling back on the bed.

"What the fuck?" Aaron said, but he was grinning, and Rob crawled up onto the bed to him and gave him the best freaking blow job of his entire goddamned life. Aaron lost the ability to talk. The sounds he made were low and almost quiet, but the way he arched up into Rob's mouth was evidence that despite everything, Rob really hadn't lost his touch.

They lay next to each other on the bed, not speaking, and Aaron closed his eyes.

"Why have we not used a bed before this?" he murmured, and then his breathing evened out, and he was asleep. Rob could throw him out now, shake him awake, tell him to leave, but he didn't. The traitorous part of him wanted to watch Aaron, see the way his whole body relaxed as he slept. He'd never wanted this to make it to a bed, wouldn't have let it if he could still get to his knees without pain the last few days.

Because if they were in a bed, then somehow, dangerously, what they had would be more than casual sex, more than friends with benefits.

It was something real.

And that terrified him.

"HEY."

The voice was close, a whisper in his ear, and Rob reached up to touch whoever was talking to him.

His body ached, but he felt relaxed; more so than he had been in a long time.

"Hey," the voice said again, and little things began to make more sense.

He ached because for the first time since the problems caused by the bullet he'd pushed through the pain to make love for real, taken his time, made things good for his lover, and not just enjoyed random fucking up against a tree.

Aaron was in bed with him.

It was daylight.

The kids!

He tried to sit up, but he was tangled up in the sheet and couldn't make his limbs work.

"It's okay," Aaron soothed and patted his chest. "Sam said he and the kids are baking. They're staying for dinner and will be back at seven."

"Sam's been here?" None of this was making sense. He was confused.

"Your phone was obnoxiously beeping at me," Aaron said and passed the phone to Rob who attempted to look at the screen, but it was all a blur. His memory was impaired, his limbs heavy, his spine cramping, and now his eyesight was blurry. He blinked to clear the fog and was finally able to read the simple words.

"Don't touch my phone again," he ordered and clutched it to his chest.

"I didn't really have a choice. I tried to wake you up but thought maybe one of the boys needed us."

"Needed *me*," Rob corrected.

"Yeah, that."

Rob wriggled to sit upright, fighting with the pillows behind his back and wincing until Aaron took pity on him and propped him up.

"So we have some time. You want me to give you a massage and loosen some of the tightness in your shoulders?"

"No." A massage was way too intimate.

"Okay then, so we can't roll around in the sack anymore. That's a given considering you look like you'd rather die than have to move."

"You could go."

Aaron pressed a hand to his chest in mock dismay. "It's like you only want me for my body."

"That's an accurate assessment." Rob knew he was an asshole, but Aaron was looking at him with fondness and care, and none of that shit sat right with him.

"So today, I saw my work partner Grace. She's having a baby, and no one knows who the father is, and it turns out she and my big brother, Saul, have been seeing each other."

Rob sighed. He didn't want to talk, and he swung his legs around. The minute the soles of his feet touched the floor, pain shot through him, and he gasped. Aaron was there in a moment, pressing fingers into his neck and talking about nothing at all.

"So Saul is all 'I'm too old,' but he's only fifty-four and fit as a fiddle, and he's spent his entire adulthood being a dad to us, so he'll make a wonderful dad to Grace's baby, and an even better husband."

The words flowed over Rob, and even though he wanted to shrug off the rhythmic press and stroke of Aaron's hands, he didn't.

"Anyway, she was at dinner today, this big family thing we have every Sunday, and we all love her, and so I'm going to be an uncle again, which is cool." His hands moved lower, and Rob tensed, leaning on the cabinet to stand up.

"That's enough."

Aaron stared up at him, and Rob had never seen anything as good as Aaron Carter in his bed. He was naked, the sheet twisted on his thighs, his cock on full view, every line of him sculptured. This was a man who worked out, who looked after himself. The kind of guy that Rob might have seen himself with.

In fact, the last few days he'd changed his mind on a lot of things.

It *was* okay to want to feel something for his nephews.

It was right for him to be proud of them. Bran with his stubborn caregiving and his love for his brother, so bright and watchful, and just like Suzi. Toby who'd come out of his shell, following Bran around like a puppy, but who smiled so much more now. He could imagine both boys growing up, and wondered if either would change.

The conflict inside him, to connect to the boys, was real. But he just had to remember that soon he'd be dead. Or if he chose the operation path and survived, then chances were he'd be paralyzed, and there was no situation where he would want to be a waste of space, dependent on others for everything.

You could do this if you had Aaron at your side.

He stumbled, watched as Aaron fought the sheet and was up by his side in an instant.

"Talk to me, Rob," he murmured as he hovered and followed Rob close to the window. "What's wrong?"

"Get dressed and get out."

"No." Aaron, it seemed, could be just as stubborn. He moved away, pulled on his clothes, then sat on the bed, which left Rob at a distinct disadvantage.

That stubbornness was so sexy, and again, as the thoughts hit him, he wondered what the hell was going on. He wanted to talk to Aaron, wanted to tell him everything, explain how he had to leave the boys, and that if he could have stayed, he could see a short-term future where he was with Aaron.

It wouldn't work for long, them being together, and God, so far it had just been sex. Still, he was feeling things that he shouldn't. A future that was alien to him, and the idea of waking up next to Aaron on a daily basis was tantalizingly out of reach.

"So Saul and Grace's wedding," Aaron began, drawing his legs up and crossing them. "You want to come with me? Be my date, like an official event where I say, 'hey, everyone, this is Bran and Toby and their uncle Rob, my boyfriend' that kind of thing?"

Rob's mouth fell open. He didn't want a boyfriend or to see him and the boys as any kind of unit.

I really want that.

He was already falling for his nephews, wanting to be there for them, even if he couldn't be. Was he destined to suffer the same miserable need to have Aaron in his life as well? He could almost taste the wedding cake, see the dancing, the laughing, and him sitting in the middle of it, unable to move, stuck in a wheelchair, maybe not able to breathe unaided.

He felt the self-pity, keenly.

Then Aaron smiled at him, and in that instant, he knew one thing. Aaron was dangerous to his heart and his life plan, and he needed to make Aaron go.

But Aaron beat him to it. He left the bed, picked up Rob's clothes, and passed them over, getting closer with each step until they were kissing, his clothes pressed between them.

And Rob didn't want to let him go.

When they parted, Aaron cupped Rob's face. "Let's get you dressed."

They ended up sitting on the back porch, the mountains beyond, the air warm, and Rob abruptly needed to hear Aaron talk some more.

"Tell me about your brothers."

Aaron reached over and twisted his fingers with Rob's.

"Saul, he's the eldest, became the dad to the other four of us when my parents died. Ryan, the youngest, he was still a baby. Next, after Saul, is Eddie, then me, then Jason, last— Ryan. Ryan's dating the actor Jordan Darby, Eddie is married to Jenny, Milly and Jake are his."

"Saul is with Grace and her baby."

Aaron squeezed his hand. "You were listening."

Rob huffed. "I didn't have a choice; you were talking *at* me."

"So Jason, he's on/off seeing this girl in the city, can't seem to pin her down. And of course, I'm with you."

He side-eyed Rob then, and his expression was clear.

I dare you to deny it.

Rob didn't have the energy to deny anything. Maybe he was *with* Aaron. Perhaps he could live this dream for a couple of days and enjoy the boys and then back the hell off before he left.

"I'm bringing my niece and nephew swimming tomorrow on my day off. You want to meet me there?"

"Maybe," Rob murmured.

Aaron stood, stretched tall. "Good, then I'll meet you at the lake."

And with a soft kiss and a promise of more, he left.

Chapter Fourteen

MILLY AND JAKE WERE ALREADY IN THE WATER, AARON watching from the bank, when Rob arrived with the boys in tow. They exchanged smiles, and the smile reached Rob's eyes, but they didn't kiss hello.

Yes, the sex last night had been off-the-charts hot. Yes, they had connected in some way, but that was for the alone times. Here, they were both uncles responsible for the kids, and they kept it to a casual brush of hands as Rob walked past to the shallows.

Aaron recalled the first time they'd met up here, Rob's nephews scared and hesitant to talk to anyone, let alone wanting to paddle in the water. But that was what they wanted now, and after he and Rob exchanged hellos, it was Rob and the kids in the shallows with Aaron watching everyone from the shore.

"Can I go out there with Milly and Jake, Uncle Rob?" Bran asked. He stared wistfully toward them.

Rob checked with Aaron. "How deep is it?"

"Not too bad. Four foot or so to the rocks, actually."

"Go on then." And before Bran could ask, Rob added a warning and then, "I've got Toby. Have fun."

When Rob and Toby came back in, Aaron handed out towels.

"One day I'll go on the rocks too," Toby announced, his hands on his hips, the towel over his head.

"You sure will, buddy," Rob said and watched when Toby disappeared into the den that the other two had already created.

"He seems a lot happier," Aaron commented and waited for the stern dismissal from Rob, the one he'd grown used to. Instead, Rob was sad, thoughtful, and gave a small shrug.

"They love Crooked Tree," he said finally. "It's a good place for them to have a home."

Hope swelled inside Aaron. Was it possible that Rob was staying and that this sexy-hot friends-with-benefit thing they had going could become something else?

"Does that mean you're staying?" he asked.

Rob shot him a glance. "The kids are," he said and stepped closer so they could talk quietly. "Not me, okay? Just the kids."

Aaron was confused. "You have to work away?" He still wasn't entirely sure what Rob did for a living. He'd never mentioned a job or that he was still in the navy. His work life was a complete blank.

"Yes."

Aaron wanted to have hope that this was true, but Rob had closed his eyes momentarily and sighed softly, which made everything that came out of his mouth after that seem like a lie.

"But you'll come back, yeah?"

"No," Rob said.

Aaron's chest tightened. He had questions, so many of them, but did he deserve to get any answers? After all, what did they have between them apart from sex? Yes, he'd fallen in lust hard, but they hadn't done anything that could be considered dating.

What about the kids? Who would be caring for them? Why wasn't Rob planning on coming back? Why would he not want to come back? Maybe he should start with a simple question, something less threatening than asking how long was Rob staying.

Milly screamed.

In a blur of movement, Rob had shallow-dived into the water and headed for the rocks, long, powerful strokes taking him directly toward the screaming.

"Stay where you are, Toby!" Aaron ordered and went in after him. By the time he reached the rocks, not that long after Rob, the screaming had stopped, but now Milly was crying.

"Bran slipped!" she shouted. "He can't stay up. I can't keep him up." Aaron immediately took over supporting Bran and assessed the situation. Bran's face was only just above water, which was only around four feet at this point, and he was deathly quiet, but his eyes were open and wide, and his breathing labored. Milly was crying. Jake tried to dive under. There was no sign of Rob down in the weeds that grew there. Jake surfaced, and Aaron decided immediately that his nephew needed to stay out of this. There was a lot of splashing, and Bran was beginning to panic.

"Stay with your sister," he demanded and then pushed his own face into the water, still trying to support Bran, checking for Rob, trying to figure out what the hell was happening. Rob was by the rocks, pulling at boulders bigger than him, and when the weeds waved around Rob's hands, Aaron saw, in the clear spring water, that somehow Bran's foot had become wedged in fallen stones.

"I'm sinking." Bran gasped and splattered as he slipped and swallowed water.

"I've got you, Bran," Aaron said.

Rob surfaced and gripped his nephew, cradled his face, and supported him alongside Aaron. "I'm getting you out," he said, the words firm. Then he turned to Aaron. "Keep his head up."

Rob duck-dived down, and Aaron supported Bran, who was gasping, his lips barely clear of the surface. He wasn't crying now, but the terror in his eyes was raw.

"It's okay, Bran. We've got you," Aaron kept repeating, even as Rob returned to the surface, took a deep breath, and dived again. Something shifted, yanking Bran momentarily under, but whatever it was didn't help because he was still held tight by the rocks below. He spluttered for a moment and then quietened again.

Rob hadn't surfaced. Milly moved closer, helped Aaron hold Bran, and she was still crying.

"Everything's okay," Aaron reassured. Should he get Milly and Jake to swim to shore? Maybe run and get help?

Finally, Rob surfaced, and he took over holding Bran.

His breathing was harsh for a while, and then he visibly reined himself in. "Bran, I need you to listen to me. You need to go under the water. Hold your breath and go under. I'll be right there with you, but your foot is twisted and stuck, and I need to get you down so I can release you. Bran? Are you listening to me?"

Bran reached up and gripped his uncle's hair, so composed, so utterly focused. "Yes."

"Okay, I need you to take some deep breaths and then one

last big one when I start to count down from three. Breathe with me, Bran."

Aaron and Rob exchanged looks.

"He's got this," Aaron said with confidence.

"Okay, Bran, on the count of three, take in a deep breath and relax for me. Don't fight me. One. Two. Three."

A split second and both he and Bran disappeared beneath the water. Milly yelped, even as Aaron decided to go under with them to check what was happening. And then, the foot was free, and Bran bobbed to the surface like a cork, with Rob soon after, holding him, carrying him over the rocks, surefooted and focused, and then slipping back into the water and swimming with Bran back to the shore. Milly and Jake scrambled to follow. Then it was only Aaron left to check they all made it back okay. When he reached the shore, Rob was sitting on the stones, Bran clinging to him like a baby monkey, sobbing, and holding on as if he would never let go. Toby joined them, and Rob held them both for the longest time.

Aaron crouched to check the foot, ran a few medical checks without making it too obvious. Bran was ominously quiet, but that didn't mean anything.

"I don't think it's broken." He said as he felt for swelling. "It's going to bruise, though. We should get back and put some ice on it."

Rob staggered to stand, bracing himself, still holding Bran and refusing to let go, and together they headed down the hill.

They all made it back to Branches. Milly had run ahead with Jake on her heels, so that when they reached the bridge, Sam and Nate were already there. Justin arrived at the same time they did.

"What happened?"

"He slipped," Aaron answered when Rob was quiet. "His foot was trapped, wedged in the boulder space. We need to get some ice on it."

"This happened before, when Justin was a kid," Nate announced. "We thought it was a freak accident. I never even thought to mention it. Shit..." He pushed a hand through his hair, then pulled himself back to the present. "Ice, we need ice."

Bran buried his face in Rob's neck, and for a few moments, Rob gripped him tight, and then he relaxed his hold.

"Sam? Can you sort the ice for Bran?"

Bran murmured something too low for Aaron to hear, and Rob shook his head.

"Go with Sam. He'll get ice for your foot."

"I want to stay with you," Bran said, louder this time.

"I can't," Rob said and unpeeled his nephew's fingers, then passed him to Justin and Sam. Justin held him, and Rob gently nudged Toby to go with them. Then, without a word, he walked in the direction of his cabin and was gone.

What just happened? Why did Rob go? No one was enlightening him, and Aaron went from confused to pissed.

He wanted to follow him, ask him what the hell was going on, but his priority was to Milly, Jake, and an injured Bran. Paramedic and uncle first. Then he could become the angry man he wanted to be. No one should push a child away, under any circumstances. His respect for what Rob had just done at the lake twisted with the feeling that something was very off.

After dropping Milly and Jake home, he was torn. Pissed at what had happened, worried about what he'd witnessed, and then angry. Mostly he was confused that he even wanted to see Rob again. Taken at face value, what he had done was awful, but wasn't he the one who'd rescued Bran, who had stayed underwater for so long?

Aaron needed a beer and a good night's sleep, but it wasn't *his* place that he ended up driving to, and it wasn't to get any sleep.

He parked under the lamp farthest from any of the buildings at Crooked Tree and then walked the short distance to Rob's cabin. The place was in complete darkness, and he made his way to the back of the building where he usually found Rob sitting. The back door was open, but inside was quiet. No sign of the kids, no sign of Rob. He went in because nothing about this felt right. The kids weren't in their bedroom, the bed empty, and he entered Rob's room.

"What do you want?" Rob asked from the shadows.

"Where are Bran and Toby? What the hell was that back there?"

Rob said nothing, and Aaron felt for the light, flicking the switch so that brightness filled the room. Two bags sat on a neatly made bed, and the closet door was open, Rob's clothes gone. And in the center of the room, hunched over in pain, Rob sat on a chair.

"I thought you would be Justin," he whispered. "I think I need to get my gun from Justin."

He looked like hell, gray, and the way he held himself, along with an unopened box of Fentanyl on the bed, underlined how much pain he was in.

Aaron's anger didn't subside, but he crossed for a closer investigation, immediately checked Rob's pulse. It was strong and steady but fast, and Rob didn't even bother moving his head.

"I took a shovel up to the lake, kept diving until I could lever the rocks apart. No child will get stuck again."

"What the hell, Rob? Why would you do that right now?"

"Because Bran and Toby have to be safe here."

Was it him, or was Rob close to tears? Jesus, what was going on here?

"I have questions." Aaron sat on the bed, to the side of Rob's chair.

"I can't," Rob murmured. His voice was tight, and pain bracketed his mouth.

"How much have you taken?" Aaron picked up the Fentanyl, realizing as he did so that it was an unopened box.

"None."

Aaron made the executive decision that whatever was going on here had to be stopped in its tracks. The prescription had Rob's name. He was in pain, so Aaron popped out the correct dosage, according to the label, and opened the bottle of water that had been discarded on the bed. He held out the pills.

"Take them," he ordered.

Rob lifted a hand, but it was maybe only an inch, and he groaned low in his throat, an animalistic sound of pain.

So Aaron took point, pressed his fingers to Rob's mouth, seeking entrance, placed the drugs on his tongue and then supported his head as he tilted the bottle. Then he waited, helping Rob by massaging his shoulders gently, pressing at the tight flesh. Had he hurt himself in the water? This was clearly an existing injury if the Fentanyl was anything to go by, so had he injured himself again? After they'd made love yesterday, he'd looked in so much pain, and right now Aaron wanted answers.

"It's not enough," Rob said a little over fifteen minutes later, able now to reach for the box, and tried to pop out two more of the small tablets. Aaron helped him, making a note of dose and calculating in his head. This was serious shit, but against his better judgment, he helped him with two more tablets. Another fifteen minutes or so, and Rob was able to move without pain.

"Start talking," Aaron demanded.

"You can leave now," Rob responded and wouldn't look at him.

"Not going anywhere. So what the hell is going on?"

"I don't owe you an explanation."

"No, you don't owe me shit, but you owe Bran and Toby one hell of a lot."

Rob winced. "They'll be okay. Justin promised to take them for me so I can…"

"So you can do what?"

This time Rob closed his eyes. "Jeez, Aaron, just go."

Aaron reached out and took Rob's hand. "No, and let's start from the beginning. The pain. Here's what I know. You're friends with Justin, so I'm taking a leap here and assuming you worked with him in the years he was missing. Maybe even that you were part of whatever Justin did that ended up with him getting shot. Right so far?" He didn't wait for the yes, merely forged ahead with his theories. "Don't forget I was the one who dug a bullet out of Justin, and I heard some things maybe I shouldn't. I know he was working for some team that worked to keep our country safe, so I assume you were in the same line of work?"

"You need to go," Rob murmured, but he didn't deny anything that Aaron had said.

"Tell me about the pain. Were you injured in the line of work? An accident? There are no visible issues I saw when I was in bed with you—"

"You fucking checked?"

Aaron was shocked to hear the horror in Rob's words.

"I kissed and licked every inch of you…" He leaned over then and stole a kiss from Rob because all the anger in him had gone. He knew something was wrong and was determined to find out what it was. Rob curled his hand into Aaron's hair and deepened the kiss, which wasn't what Aaron had been expecting.

"You don't know me." Rob was tired, and he hunched forward in the chair again.

"What? You mean some of the things you did for your family? What you saw, who you killed? You forget I was a soldier for a lot of years."

Rob huffed a quick laugh. "Your job was to save lives. My targets never got up again." He stopped then as if he realized he had said too much.

"Shades of gray, Rob, always shades of gray. How many targets did you take out that would have gone on to hurt other people."

"That's too fucking simplistic. You're wrong if you think I can even tell you that."

"Can you ever come to terms with what you did? Is this why you won't talk about it?"

Rob grabbed his hand and held tight. "Come to terms with it? I regret nothing. I chose to be the surgeon here. I wasn't lied to, not like Justin was. I was young, idealistic, and I wanted to make the country I lived in safer. I didn't hurt a single person who wasn't going to hurt someone else, and I saved lives. None of it haunts me, okay, so don't try to psychoanalyze the shit out of me. I'm not the victim here, and I don't need *understanding*."

Aaron didn't doubt a single word of it. He'd signed up to the army to save lives, but he'd left because he hadn't been able to save enough. He'd come to terms with his own ghosts. At least he had coping mechanisms to keep them at bay. He'd met too men and women who carried demons from war at Hepburn House, and who couldn't let those demons free.

Rob sighed noisily. "I can see you are thinking about how fucked I am in the head, but it's all about checks and balances for me. For every person I surgically removed, maybe the team I was with saved another or ten or a hundred. You'll have to get Justin to tell you about the bomb meant for a football stadium. We stopped that."

"Okay," Aaron murmured. "Then if ghosts aren't chasing you away, why are you leaving like a thief in the night? Why leave the boys?"

"You think I *want* to leave them? I have to leave before they form any attachment to me that will end up hurting them."

Aaron recalled the way Bran clung to Rob. "I think maybe you're too late for that."

Silence. Too much silence. And then Rob began to speak again.

"I really wish I'd met you sooner," Rob whispered. "I think we could have been good together."

That all sounded very final, and Aaron didn't like it. "We still can be."

"No, you don't get it." He scrubbed his eyes. "Why would you? It's not like I've told you anything." He muttered the last bit.

Aaron leaned in. "You want to start again?"

"I only have maybe two months left." He was more explicit this time, and the words were icily hard.

Aaron heard the words but they didn't make sense. Was Rob being sent on a clandestine mission? Was his war still happening? If it was, then there was the possibility that he could come back. He'd made it alive this far, so why would it be any different?

"Until what? Deployment? A mission?"

Rob looked thoughtful, then shook his head. "Did you

know, and I read this on Google, so it must be true, that there are less than one hundred reported cases of lead toxicity in patients with retained bullets? And I'm the lucky one to take that total closer to a hundred."

Aaron heard the words but couldn't process them immediately, and then it hit him.

"You were shot, and the bullet is still inside you."

"Yep, it went in through my side, struck a rib, and the trajectory changed. I mean, it was lucky it hit a rib because that meant my internal organs were missed. Still, it stayed close to my spine, and there it sits right in a mess of severely damaged muscles and scar tissue."

Aaron had seen that kind of thing before. On the battlefield, there was no chance of extricating a bullet. The patient needed delicate surgery, but that didn't mean the bullet couldn't be taken out. The moment a victim's vitals were stabilized, even in the middle of being fired on, a medics first response is to determine trajectory, counting entry and exit holes, and imagining the path of the bullet. Aaron could visualize the kind of path that Rob was describing.

"So in two months, you're having it taken out? You can still come back after."

"To what exactly?"

"To the kids. To me?"

"You? I don't have anything for *you*."

"Rob—"

"You know when a stone cracks a windshield, how the spider web of cracks spread outward from the impact? Well, my doctor said that's what happened to the muscles in my back. You can't see it on the surface, but the damage is inside."

"But the fragments can come out," Aaron insisted. He'd

seen it done. With average results, maybe, but it *had* been done.

"When the doctors told me what had happened, my first thought was that I wished I'd died because then there wouldn't be the pain, and anyway, me dying there and then mattered to no one. I argued with them to take the bullet out. Particularly when they told me there was going to be a creeping paralysis and poisoning from the bullet fragments leaching lead. They told me I had two options. Stay with the bullet in me, live with the pain, and eventually die. Or have the operation, possibly die, but if I lived, I could potentially be paralyzed. So I decided to leave the hospital."

"And live with the pain until you die." Aaron could understand that. Long-term pain management could be done.

"It's getting worse. Faster than they said it would, and I refuse to decay slowly in some hospital room from poisoning or paralyzed after an operation, with my only family watching me die. They've lost their dad, their mom, I refuse to let them see me die as well. So, I'm dying on my terms and sparing everyone the grief of watching it happen."

Aaron sat back. "That's why you want your gun back?"

Rob nodded.

"What kind of a man with a family gives up?" Aaron snapped the words out. Bran and Toby needed their uncle.

"I'm not their family. I want to be, but I can't. You see that, right?"

"No, it's not just about blood. I see you with them. You don't want to leave them."

"I have to, which is why I am finding a family to look after them."

Aaron stopped for a moment, lost in thought.

"What about us?" he asked sadly.

This time it was Rob sitting back in his chair, the meds having worked their magic, it seemed. "What about us?"

Aaron wanted to shout at Rob, to tell him he was wrong, to change his mind and at least give the operation a chance, but he was selfish. What right did he have to make someone have an operation that might paralyze them? How could he sit here and say that it was okay to be slowly poisoned and that pain could be dealt with?

He didn't do any of that.

"How about you get some sleep, right? Then we can talk this over together, in the morning."

Rob used the chair to balance himself, then crawled onto the bed and lay down, his back to Aaron.

"Lock the door on the way out."

Aaron did lock the door, but not with him outside. He wasn't leaving Rob, not when he was in pain.

Not when there is a chance I can change his mind.

He slid into the bed behind Rob and pulled the covers around them. Rob didn't move or give any sign he even knew Aaron was still there, and with Aaron's hand on Rob's hip, touching him for reassurance that he was still there, still alive, he slept.

SUNLIGHT SHONE DIRECT into Aaron's eyes.

Locking the door was one thing, but maybe he should have pulled the drapes while he'd been at it.

He reached out to touch Rob and felt nothing but cold sheets. He knew with absolute certainty that there was no point in checking the cabin. Or even the whole of Crooked Tree.

Rob was gone.

Chapter Fifteen

ROB WAS IN HIS CAR AT FOUR A.M. HIS BAGS IN THE TRUNK, and he was ready to head out. He hadn't managed to get his gun back from Justin. There was no point in even trying, so he'd have to rethink his strategy, and go back to the idea of swallowing a couple of boxes of Fentanyl.

Of course, first off, he needed to get away from Crooked Tree, and that in itself wasn't going to be easy. He'd already had to use every stealthy side of himself to get out from under Aaron grip, which had started gentle and ended up being a tight hold of his shirt.

Something smacked the hood of the car, and Rob jumped.

Justin stood there, arms crossed over his chest and chin jutted with stubborn determination. He stalked around to the passenger door and got in.

"Do you ever sleep?" Rob asked.

"I knew you were going to leave after yesterday." Justin's tone was even as he shut the door.

What the hell?

He wasn't surprised at the fact Justin was there. He was stunned, however, when Justin threw a familiar bag onto the back seat. That was Justin's go bag, the pick-and-run items for when they needed to get somewhere fast.

"I'm going with you," he announced and belted up.

"No, you're not."

"I'm assuming you'll want to avoid your body being found after you kill yourself? Or maybe you do want it found? Maybe you want to make it look like an accident, so your nephews will have closure?"

"Justin—"

"That's why I'm here. I'll help you, call it payback for the fact you didn't shoot me when you were at Crooked Tree before and that you arranged things so I could be with Sam without fear of reprisals."

"I don't need you with me."

Justin lifted his jacket and pulled out a gun from the holster—Rob's gun—sliding it into the glovebox. "Thought you might want that."

He then settled back in the seat.

"You need to… Sam… you have. Fuck, I'm leaving Bran and Toby with you."

"And?" Justin asked and side-eyed him.

"I don't want you anywhere near me when I do this. None of what happens can get back to the kids, okay? You need to get out of the damn car."

Justin folded his arms over his chest and shrugged. "Make me."

Rob considered the options. Justin was fit; Rob wasn't. Justin was a stubborn fucker on a mission. Rob was in a messy state of what-ifs and maybe's, and it didn't help he'd be leaving the kids behind and had left Aaron warm in bed.

"I hate you," he snapped.

"Not as much as I hate you," Justin replied, steadily.

Rob started the engine and pulled out of the parking area, heading away from Crooked Tree and then north.

"We probably need a large city," Justin mused. "Maybe you can pull your gun out at a mall or something, suicide by cop. Or how about we go to a river, you can shoot yourself, and I'll push you into the water. Thing is both those things are shit, aren't they? If a cop kills you, then think of his family and what he has to live with. What if it was Ryan who had to shoot you? Imagine the pain and how it would touch his family."

"I'm not involving anyone else in this."

"Well, you are, actually. You're involving me. I'm here in the car with you."

"I never asked you to get into the damn car."

"I never asked you to dump your nephews on me. What if Sam and I don't want a family? Worse, what if we wanted our own family, and now we've been left with kids we don't know?"

Rob pulled the car over into a picnic area surrounded by trees, and killed the engine, abruptly, overwhelmingly lost for what to say. "You said it was okay."

Justin turned in his seat. "You didn't leave me much choice."

"I did."

"You want a family for them. Well, they've got a family. You."

"I don't have much time left."

"You have the operation. You don't know how much time you have left."

"I won't do that, J. I refuse to become something to be pitied and ignored, a burden to the kids, or someone who lives a long life strapped to a bed."

"Still," Justin mused, then opened the glovebox and

pulled out the gun, checking the chamber and releasing the safety. "I don't think it matters how you take yourself out. It will still be me and Sam picking up the pieces." He held out the gun to Rob. "Do it here. I'll take care of the body."

Rob hesitated and then took his Glock, the heft of it reassuring but cold in his hand.

"Okay," he murmured.

"It's just a shame, you know," Justin mused, as if something had only just occurred to him.

"What?"

"When I came back to Crooked Tree I was ready to die as well." He huffed a laugh. "It's a fucked up world we live in where the two of us would rather take death over the second chance that Crooked Tree could give us."

"You actually have a future that I can't hope for anymore."

Justin shrugged. "Whatever."

They were quiet for a while.

"What will you tell Bran and Toby when I'm gone?"

Justin shook his head. "Is that only just occurring to you?"

"I never got much past leaving them. I thought I would have time to think, but I don't."

"Whatever." Justin repeated, then released his belt and indicated they get out of the car. "We should go into the woods some."

Rob climbed out and pocketed the gun, waiting for Justin, until both of them walked up the path that apparently led to somewhere called Hummers Lookout. Neither of them stopped until they reached the top. The lookout offered a view over a vast lake, a reservoir fed by mountain springs, high-sided, and with a guardrail that warned of rockfalls and deep water. Rob shouldn't have noticed how beautiful it was, but he did—every minute detail.

"Seems like as good a place as any," Justin mused and peered over the edge at the water below. "But we need to get on with it. Bran's ankle is swollen, and Sam wants to take him to the hospital, get an X-ray."

Rob clenched the gun. "What? Is Bran okay?"

"I'm sure he will be. You should have heard him last night, talking about you and how you saved him." Justin leaned on the fence and stared into the distance. "It will be a good memory for him."

They stood in silence. Rob was lost in thought as he watched the day brighten around him. He didn't know what the time was, but no doubt the boys would be up by now, and as for Aaron? He would have realized that Rob had gone. He imagined, somewhere in the mess of everything, that the kids had changed him. It seemed he was easily persuaded by tears and smiles and hugs and by the way they looked at him as if he hung the moon and the stars. Gone was the suspicion and defensiveness, and now they wanted his help.

He'd been so confident that the best thing for everyone was to take himself out of the equation, not be a burden, but how fucking selfish was that now?

Standing here staring at the mountains, the sunlight creeping across the land in bright swathes on the water, he realized his decision didn't seem so cut-and-dried. He'd spent his entire life not forming attachments for one good reason— it would hurt too much to lose them. But now, he wasn't so hard and forceful and focused on avoiding connection.

After all, look at the way he hugged his nephews when they cried. Or the way he'd let Aaron creep into his life. Hell, see how he'd let the kids *and* Aaron into his heart? His eyes burned, and his throat was tight. Could he live for the people who depended on him now?

I'm scared.

Fuck my life.

He pressed the fingers of his spare hand to his temple and massaged the pressure point, all the while holding the gun tight, the safety off, the window for decisions slowly closing. Finally, unbidden, he flicked on the safety and pocketed the gun.

Justin sighed noisily.

"Now can we go home?"

They walked back down to the car in companionable silence, but it was Justin who took the keys from him after deciding Rob was in no fit state to drive. He was right. Rob was shaky and emotional, and all of the things he'd never been before.

Justin started the engine but then reached into his pocket, pulling the bullets out he'd clearly never even put into Rob's gun. They sat evil and gray in Justin's open hand.

Rob closed his eyes. He hadn't even noticed there were no bullets, hell, he knew the weight of the weapon with and without bullets.

Normally.

"You have to realize you're not alone," Justin said. "Someone in this world wanted you to live. It might have just been me up on that hill, but it's not just me in the rest of your life, is it?" He pushed the bullets back into his pocket, and Rob didn't have anything he could say.

When they reached Crooked Tree, he headed straight for Sam and Justin's place, climbing the stairs and opening his arms as soon as he saw his nephews.

Toby threw himself across the room, and Rob braced

himself to catch him, with Bran sedately walking toward him, with no sign of a limp, desperate for a hug.

"Are you okay?" Bran asked when they separated. "Sam said you were sore from yesterday."

Rob caught Sam's gaze, gave a small nod in thanks. "I was, but I'm all good now. Have you guys had breakfast?"

"Nope, we was waitin' for you," Toby lisped, "an' look, I lost my tooth, but the fairy isn't at this house, Justin said they hate tents."

Rob saw the campout that Justin and Sam had created for the kids, cushions and blankets, and a whole mess of cuddly toys. Where they'd come from, he didn't know, but a closer look showed they were all soft horses with the Crooked Tree logo on them.

"What did you guys do?" he asked Sam. "Raid the entire shop?"

Sam wrinkled his nose. "I wanted the boys to be cozy."

"The bill is in the mail," Justin added.

Rob walked into Justin and Sam's bedroom, Justin following, and handed over the gun.

"Put it away, please."

Then he scooped up Toby, who was still chattering on about the tooth fairy, and Bran took his hand. Together, they made their way down to Branches, choosing their usual table. They ordered everything, or so it seemed to Rob, but he didn't care, because hell, he was still in shock. He'd made the decision not to end things today, but did that mean he was only waiting until there was another point where leaving the boys seemed right?

And what about Aaron? Would he be able to leave Aaron as well?

The door opened, and Aaron stepped in. He was frowning, his lips in a thin line, but when he spotted Rob, it was as if the worry lifted immediately. He crossed to their table and took the empty seat, just as he had done that first time. Close up he looked like hell, and guilt knifed Rob's gut.

"You're still here," Aaron stated, his voice tight. "I thought you were…"

"Coffee?" Rob asked and passed the pot.

Aaron stared at him in disbelief and then filled his mug.

"What happened?" he said quietly. The boys were comparing stuffed horses and seemed oblivious to the tension in the room.

"I'm here, for now," Rob murmured and saw the flash of disappointment on Aaron's face. He knew that Aaron probably wanted him to announce he was taking himself off to the hospital to get himself operated on. But he wasn't ready for that, nor did he think he ever would be.

"Okay," Aaron sipped his coffee and listened to the tooth fairy story, but every so often he glanced over at Rob, and the sadness never left his eyes.

THE DAY WAS like any other. Nothing remained of the morning where Rob had made a life-changing decision. He walked up to the lake with the boys, but understandably Bran was cautious about swimming out so far, and it took a while before he could get Toby into the water. They worked on swimming skills, and by the time they'd finished, Rob needed painkillers and a good hot shower.

"Hey, who wants to help me feed the horses?" Luke called as they passed the barns.

And just like that, Rob was on his own and heading back to the cabin with the promise that Luke would also take the boys to a Todd family barbecue celebrating Ashley's birthday, adding the option of a sleepover, which was apparently Justin's idea. Go figure.

Rob was invited, not to the sleepover of course, but to the party. He cried off, explaining he'd hurt his back in the water yesterday, already planning on what he needed to do now. He had hours to spare, and he reached the cabin but didn't go inside. Instead, he got into his car. He dry-swallowed Tylenol and pulled out his phone, googling a number for Carters, which was the only connection to Aaron he could think of.

"This is Rob, from Crooked Tree. I need to see Aaron," he said as soon as he connected to Carters. He didn't know who he was talking to, didn't really care, but whoever it was asked him his name and then easily passed over an address.

"Tell him Saul sent you."

The house was small, probably a two-bedroom, but old in style, the yard a wild mess of color and just this side of tamed. There was an old Toyota in the drive, evidence that Aaron's car was here, even if he wasn't.

The door opened before he reached it, and Aaron leaned on the doorjamb.

"Saul called me," he said before Rob could get his words out.

"I thought we could talk?" Jeez, he sounded so uncertain, and he cleared his throat. "We need to talk."

"About what?"

"Are you going to let me in?"

Aaron moved to one side, and Rob walked in, past the man who was messing with his head, and into the cool interior. The August day was hot, and he needed some shade and a drink.

It seemed as if Aaron was on the same wavelength, offering beer and cold water. Rob took the water and waited for Aaron to tell them where they were going. After a moment's pause, he inclined his head and left the kitchen, going down the hall to another door and pushing into the bedroom.

"I said we need to talk." Rob balked at going in because he knew he plus Aaron plus bed would likely end up in more than they needed to be doing.

"Take off your shirt," Aaron said and turned his back to Rob, rummaging in a drawer. He pulled out a jar of massage cream and unscrewed the lid, turning back to Rob and frowning when he saw Rob hadn't moved. "Come on, take it off, and your belt, loosen your jeans. No, that isn't enough. Take it all off. Strip."

Rob limped to the bed and did as instructed, except for keeping on his boxers. So much for talking.

"You look like shit," Aaron murmured and then helped Rob to lie on his belly. "At the same time... look at that body."

Rob made a move to get up.

"I was joking," Aaron said, with a hand on Rob's lower back. "Well, no I wasn't, but I'm a medic. I can avoid sex if I need to. Of course, I'm lying about that, too."

Rob moved the pillow so he could support his face and not asphyxiate; the pillow smelled of Aaron, that particular mix of soap and scent that made him hard in his pants.

"What vertebrae are the fragments lodged against?"

"T5."

"Okay, I'll concentrate on your shoulders and lower back. It's where you're carrying all your pain. I have acupuncture needles as well."

Rob couldn't argue, didn't want to. He was tired, and Aaron had his hands on him, the scent of lotion in his nostrils, and the rhythmic press and pull of a gentle massage. Aaron found all the bad points, the places where there was referred pain because he held himself so stiffly right now. They hurt but eased, and the needles were pinpoint sharp, and his muscles fought them. Slowly he began to relax and listened to Aaron breathe, the slow inhale and exhale, imagining the feel of it on his heated skin.

"You need this every day," Aaron murmured, smoothing hands to the base of Rob's spine, the weight of him down by Rob's knees as he straddled him. With each pass, they moved closer to his ass, and Aaron eased down his boxers until they were hooked beneath the globes of his ass and on his erection, which wouldn't dissipate much as he tried to think about all the nasty things he'd seen in his life. "Right after we make love again."

"We never have," Rob said, his words not making sense, his mind blurry. "We had sex."

Aaron chuckled, then pressed against a particularly hard knot, keeping his touch there, firm, until the muscle eased a little.

"You were having sex. I was falling for you."

"You... can't..."

"Telling me I can't, doesn't mean it isn't true."

"I don't—" Rob was going to say that he didn't have any affection for Aaron, that his friend with benefits was nothing more than that.

I'd be lying. I want more than sex. I want the kids as my family, and I want to make love with Aaron, and be a kind of father, and I hate that I can't. Emotion pressed his chest, and for a moment he couldn't breathe.

"Did you ask Justin about the boys?"

The question pulled him back off the edge. "Huh?"

"Sam said he and you went for a drive, when I woke up and you were gone. Did you tell him about the bullet and ask him to take Bran and Toby."

What was the point of lying to Aaron? "More than that. Justin already knew most of it, but he talked me off the edge."

There was a pause, Aaron's talented hands moving to his hips and the muscles to the side of his back.

"I'll be there for them, too," Aaron said, and then Rob felt the brush of his hair on sensitive skin as Aaron leaned over to kiss the back of his neck. "For you, I'll look out for them."

Rob sighed, another piece of stone weighing him down falling to the ground, shattering into a million tiny pieces.

"Thank you." Maybe it was the silence or the scent or Aaron's hands on him, but tears welled in his eyes, and as much as he wanted them to go away, they weren't going anytime soon.

"There," Aaron announced, pressing another kiss where he had before. "Close your eyes and get some sleep."

And miraculously, that was exactly what Rob did.

Chapter Sixteen

AARON EASED OFF ROB, LYING TO ONE SIDE AND WATCHING
the man who'd stolen his heart sleeping. He had incredibly
long lashes, beautiful, thick, and Aaron could imagine the
deep green that lay beneath. Full of secrets, Rob was an
enigma.

He left the room a couple of times, to use the bathroom,
to get another drink, but each time he crawled back onto the
bed and lay next to him. Just because Rob hadn't left this
morning didn't mean he wouldn't vanish altogether. He was
adamant he was done, that there was nothing left, and the
grief that carved inside Aaron stole his breath.

His job was to save lives and dispatch to people who
could care and nurture and make his patients whole. But with
Rob, he wanted to do that. He wanted to make him see there
could be a chance.

When Rob woke, he was facing Aaron. His eyelashes
fluttered and then closed.

"Are you watching me?" he asked and turned to face the
other way.

"Absolutely," Aaron said and ran a finger down Rob's

spine, pausing briefly over T5 but not so much that Rob would feel it.

"That's creepy."

"Whatever."

Rob turned his head on the pillow, and this time his eyes were open, and the green was intense with emotion.

Aaron reached for him, cupping his face and kissing him. The angle was awkward, but Rob moved as well, rolling to lie on Aaron, and deepen the kisses.

And just like that, passion took them, and there was no second when Rob would let him pause or worry about his back or make any attempt at conversation. Rob was naked, and Aaron still wore his jeans and a T, but he made short work of that, or as quick as it could be when he didn't want to break the kissing.

"Condoms? Lube?" Rob asked.

Aaron pointed at the drawer. "In there."

Rob pulled the drawer hard, awkward on the bed, and cursed when it didn't open immediately.

"I want you to..." Rob said, passing the things to Aaron and waiting.

"I don't think..." Aaron had a lot to say about pain management and need being diametrically opposed, but then Rob kissed him, and he knew there was only one way to do this. He arranged Rob on his back, spent a while licking and sucking Rob's erection, which made Rob demand more.

"Stay there," he ordered. Then added more gently, "Promise me something."

"What?"

"If your back hurts, you need to tell me. We don't have to do this."

Rob reached up and tangled a hand in Aaron's hair. "Yes, we do, Army."

Aaron hurried to strip off, squeezing lube onto his fingers and positioning himself so Rob could see him stretching himself. Rob reached for him, closed a hand around his cock, and moved it in time to the press inside, and suddenly Aaron wasn't sure exactly how long he'd last if they didn't get on with this quickly.

He wiped his hands on his discarded T-shirt and hurried to open a condom, but Rob took it off him, smoothing it over his cock and fisting himself.

"Are you sure? I can—"

Aaron cut off whatever Rob was going to say with a kiss, and then he lowered himself onto Rob.

"Wait," Aaron paused, licking his way into Rob's mouth, taking every taste he could, waiting for his body to relax, swallowing the soft groan of approval from Rob.

"Please..."

Aaron kissed away the plea and began to move, his breathing heavy. Slowly, firmly he rose and sunk back again, and through all of it, Rob never shut his eyes.

"I'm so close," Rob warned, reaching up to cup Aaron's face, drawing him down to kiss. They carried on a little longer. Then Aaron used a hand on himself, timing it to the erratic beat of Rob's heart, and then finally, abruptly, Rob was coming, and Aaron twisted his hand, deliciously on edge, and painted Rob's chest with white.

For a while, Aaron stayed still. Then somehow, they separated, Rob dealing with the condom, and then both of them lay back on the bed.

This was it. In Aaron's mind, they had made love. What was Rob thinking? When Rob curled a hand into his and laced their fingers, he knew for certain this was more than just sex.

"The boys. You. All of you make me want more," Rob murmured.

And that was all Aaron wanted to hear.

ROB MUST HAVE SLEPT; a low dose of Fentanyl and the massage had taken the edge off the pain enough for him to at least close his eyes again. The next Aaron knew, he blinked his eyes open, and it was dark, Rob snuggling into his side and an arm casually over Aaron's stomach.

He really should wake Rob up.

In a minute. No rush just yet.

THE NEXT TIME AARON WOKE, he was confused. He didn't realize at first what had woken him, and then he realized it wasn't a natural awakening, but Rob kissing his way down Aaron's body, spending time nibbling and tugging on his nipples, cupping his balls, licking and sucking his cock. Every touch was electric, but Aaron lay still. Until Rob moved to face the other way and abruptly, in the half dark, Aaron was met with a decision whether to suck Rob as Rob was doing to him. No brainer really.

For the second time, when they were done, he slept again, but this time he placed a hand over Rob's, which rested on his belly, and everything felt a little less *wrong.*

WHEN HE WOKE TO DAYLIGHT, Rob was sat on the bed next to him.

"I have to go. I said I'd teach Bran how to dive." Rob gave him one last long-lingering kiss, the kind that rocked

Aaron to his core, and finished it off with cradling Aaron's face and smoothing his thumbs under Aaron's eyes.

Aaron was concerned. "Are you sure that's a good idea?"

"I just want to give him one more memory." They kissed again. "You're an addiction," he murmured. "I wish I had time for more memories with you." Then he was gone, and the pain in Aaron's heart was enough to steal his breath.

Chapter Seventeen

Rob had become domesticated. Even more so when Aaron left a toothbrush at the cabin, followed by a shaver, clothes, and a pile of books he wanted to read. Rob never commented on it, but two weeks after that first massage, he was getting them every day, sometimes twice a day, and he felt more comfortable as if the cracks in his muscles were easing and vanishing. Of course, they weren't, and the bullet was still there, but he could almost forget it. Aaron was part of his life.

But not as much as Bran and Toby were.

This morning had demonstrated precisely how they depended on him because when they were bickering over the last pancake, he'd told them to quit it. Dad-like. And they blinked at him before exchanging broad grins.

"Whatever," he muttered, but he did make another pancake to stop the arguments.

Getting soft in your old age, Rob.

When the pain became too much for massages and painkillers to handle, it was the beginning of the end, but he focused on living his life in the now, with Aaron and the kids.

That first day had turned into two, and a week into ten days, and he still hadn't left the kids at Crooked Tree. Leaving had been on his radar, but that meant throwing away the kids' trust in him and how much they loved Aaron and how strong they were as a four.

He had to leave now while he still could, but he had two options.

Vanish as he had first imagined he would do. Take himself out of the equation, so he wasn't a burden. That was option one.

The second option was scarier.

Have the operation.

He'd considered having it away from there, working through it, not being a burden, then coming back if he was able to.

"You stopped reading," Toby announced and elbowed him in the stomach, which was enough to snap him out of the turmoil in his head. "The teddy is in the box, and?"

Toby had a fierce expression on his face, not exactly the sleepy child he was supposed to be after a bath and a bedtime story. Maybe that had something to do with the fact that this story dealt with a teddy put in a box in the attic by parents after their children had grown up. At least that is what Rob read between the lines. He really should have checked the story before he started it. Then he wouldn't have Toby glaring up at him, but Luke had handed over a whole pile of books, and he assumed they'd be okay.

"Make it okay," Toby demanded.

He turned the page and was relieved to see a picture of the teddy climbing out of the box. Toby relaxed then, cuddling into his side, smelling of soap and powder, Bunny between them, and waited for more.

When the book was done, and Toby's eyelids had grown

heavy, Rob looked for Aaron, who had vanished into the kitchen threatening to make the best hot chocolate known to man for Bran. He hadn't come back yet, but the weakness in his arms meant he wasn't able to carry a sleeping boy to bed.

Even though he desperately wanted to.

Toby fell asleep in his arms, and Rob closed his eyes for a moment, savoring the fact his nephew trusted him this much and believed however much a teddy was in an attic, unloved, that Rob could make it right. He must have dozed off as well, the weight and warmth of Toby enough to relax him. Of course, the meds helped, taking the edge of most of the pain, but was now at the point where it wasn't working as well as it should. He was losing the strength in his right arm and leg, his balance was shaky, and the headaches were rough.

I'm losing the ability to hold the boys. To be their hero. Does it matter if I died on the operating table? I would still be unable to hold them. Paralysis though, I'd be in a chair, but I could still read to them. And I'd have Aaron?

Aaron appeared then and reached down to take Toby, smiling at Rob and taking the little boy to bed. When he came back, he slumped in the chair opposite and sighed noisily.

"Twenty-one," he announced.

"Twenty-one what?"

"Itsby bitsy tiny marshmallows in the mug. We balanced twenty-one of them, glued with cream."

Rob blinked at his lover. "You gave Bran all that sugar before bed?"

"Of course not. Do I look stupid? I ate them all."

"So now I have to deal with a hyperactive adult instead."

Aaron patted his flat belly. "I can handle my sugar," he said and then leered at Rob. "We'll work it off."

Rob shook his head. "Not tonight. I'm sorry."

That had Aaron sitting up, alert. "Is the pain too much? Do you need me to use the needles—?"

"No, I want to talk."

Aaron didn't slump back, but his expression changed, became wary. "I won't let you leave to go somewhere to die," he announced, his hands in fists. "I love you, and I will follow you and stop you."

Rob had no doubt that was true. "I love you, too." There, he'd said it, and he meant it, and Aaron's mouth fell open. "I love the boys, I want to be a dad to them, and I love you."

Aaron moved then, kneeling in front of Rob, so many questions waiting to tumble out of him.

"What happened?"

"Toby trusted me to save the teddy, and Bran asked me to show him how to shave so he would know well in advance. And you…"

"What about me?" Aaron glanced at him suspiciously.

"You make me think that all of this could be real."

"It can be."

"What if I'm paralyzed? What if we can't make love? What if this is us done and you end up as my carer? I don't know if I can do that to you or the kids."

Aaron rested his hands on Rob's knee.

"I've only loved one other man, you know. His name was Elijah, and he was another medic. It was flash-fire fast, more lust than love at first, all done on the quiet, no future for us. Everything was bleak, but we finally said that we loved each other. He only lived another week after that. An IED took out our transport, and he died in my arms." He paused. "You want to know something? There wasn't a scratch on me, and I was desperate to die alongside him. I was trapped out there. I'd lost the only brightness in my days, and I never re-enlisted. That was six years ago. I've come to think that I was lucky to have him for as long as I did, but if he'd survived, lost a limb, suffered head injury, I wouldn't have loved him any less."

Rob closed his hand over Aaron's. "That was some speech."

Aaron smiled at him, and the humor reached his eyes. "Whatever happens, we'll deal with it together. I'm not naive, I know it's not as easy as getting ramps installed, or working through the pain. But, I won't ever leave you to deal with this alone. So, you have to promise me this; Don't let the past steal your future. Our future. You, me, and the boys, and maybe a girl or two."

"What?"

"I'm one of five. I like big families."

Then he grinned, and Rob knew he was teasing, but the thought of more children, of life beyond today, was exciting and shiny, and he abruptly wanted it so bad that he could only really make one choice.

"I spoke to Doctor Maynard today. He wants me to come in. Aaron, tomorrow, will you drive me to the hospital?"

Aaron sat up and kissed him deeply, then pulled back, and his eyes were bright with emotion.

"God, yes."

DOCTOR MAYNARD SMILED at them when they walked in. That was a good sign, right? He wouldn't be smiling if he was going to hand over a load of bad news. He held out his hand, and they shook.

"This is Aaron Carter, my…" Rob didn't know what to call Aaron.

"Rob's partner," Aaron said with confidence and held out

a hand which the doctor shook. He was still smiling. In fact, he had dimples, which went nicely with silver-white hair and a neat goatee, which was disconcerting to find attractive on a man who had to be close to retiring.

Doctor Maynard pulled a file in front of him. "I'm so pleased you came in." Rob and Aaron sat, and then everything passed in a blur. Aaron had questions, asked them with the authority of someone who had medical knowledge, and Rob began to tune out the back and forth, staring out at the parking lot and wondering all over again what the hell he was doing here.

For Bran and Toby.

For Aaron.

For me.

"...Type I, transfixing with small fragments inside the canal... computed tomography is the next test... accurate location of the bullet, definition of bone damage and the presence of intracanal fragments... evaluation of instability... intravenous broad-spectrum antibiotic therapy seven to fourteen days..."

The words all ran into each other, but he tried his hardest to look interested. He'd gotten to the point where this worked. Or it didn't. What else could happen?

Aaron took his hand and squeezed, and Rob came back into the room and imagined he'd missed something vital.

"Huh?" he asked.

"Doc was explaining that removal of the fragments might not resolve all of the pain, but it can be managed with tricyclic antidepressants and anticonvulsants."

"Such as amitriptyline or gabapentin," the doctor finished, and Aaron was nodding along in agreement.

Only one thing was in Rob's thoughts, quite apart from

managing any possible pain. "If I live, will I be able to move? After, I mean."

"Surgery will be performed by myself and Doctor Trevor McArthur, an orthopedic surgeon and at the top of his field."

"But that doesn't answer my question," Rob prodded.

"Full recovery is possible," the doctor began, his expression serious. "Also full paraplegia, or paralysis below the waist, is possible. Then there could be anything in between."

At least he wasn't sugarcoating all of this, so the ball was now very firmly in Rob's court.

"I want to go home," Rob announced over the two of them talking about acute care facilities and discharge.

Aaron turned to him straight away. "Rob, no, you decided you were doing this. We should talk some more, if you have any doubts…"

"None," Rob murmured. "I don't mean I want to go home forever. Book me in. I want to go home and say goodbye to the kids properly and explain a little about what is happening. I need to do that first. Okay?"

His head hurt, and he wanted to sleep, which is what he did when he got into the car. He slept all the way back to Crooked Tree and for the remainder of the afternoon.

Sitting with the boys and explaining what was happening was something he never wanted to do ever again. Not even with Aaron there as his backup.

"Mom went into the hospital and didn't come out," Toby cried.

This is what I was afraid of.

I should have left when I could.

Rob opened his arms, and Toby climbed onto his lap, burying his face into the soft fabric of Rob's shirt.

"I promise I will try my hardest to come home," he said, but that was the wrong thing to say.

"Didn't Mom try then? Is that why she died?" Bran was dry-eyed. He hadn't shed a single tear, just pulled back his shoulders and sat stoically on the end of the sofa.

"Of course she tried," Aaron tried to explain, but Rob held up a hand to stop him.

"Your mom was so strong, and she loved you more than anything. So much that she made sure there was someone to look after you if the cancer was too much." He was lying now because what she'd done was name *him*, but the truth was that he knew her, and she would have fought every single step of the way.

"You didn't come for a whole year," Bran accused, but he did stand up and looked as if he might join Toby and Rob in the soft recliner.

There was no defense for what he'd done, cutting himself off from Suzi and the boys. He thought he'd been doing the right thing, not infecting them with the terror he saw, not putting them in danger, but every day he lived with Toby and Bran he doubted his conviction.

"All I can say is sorry," he offered and waited for the response.

Bran didn't say anything, but he did perch on the side of the chair and leaned against his uncle. That was step one.

Toby fell asleep a little later, and Aaron was the one who put them to bed.

"What will happen to us if you don't come back?" Bran asked, sitting upright in bed. "We won't go back to places where the dads shout at us all the time. We'll run away and live in a tent at Silver Lake."

"You'll have me," Aaron murmured and tousled Bran's hair.

Rob wanted to add to that. "Crooked Tree has so many families, and there will be one here for you. That I *can* promise."

Bran nodded and snuggled under the covers. "We'll come and visit every day," he announced sleepily, "even if we have to catch the bus like we did with Mom."

"We'll stay near your uncle," Aaron said, and that seemed to be enough to pacify Bran, and finally he closed his eyes.

Rob went into the kitchen but couldn't recall why he'd been heading that way. This was a known side effect from the lead in his spine, a general feeling of disconnection, and some major headaches. He didn't have the energy tonight.

But he let Aaron guide him to bed to sleep, and that was enough.

———

THE CAR RIDE to the hospital was quiet. Aaron had to drive of course, which meant Rob had plenty of thinking time.

He had to channel his determination to get things done, his ability to fight against the odds, and then come back for the boys, be an uncle to them for real. This was a risk worth taking.

It had to be.

He was resigned to it all, which should have made things easier, but he also felt sick to his stomach with fear. Not that he would ever tell anyone that. Not even Aaron.

Justin had hugged him this morning. Wished him luck. Promised he would be there for Bran and Toby, and that was all Rob could ask for.

Only he wanted more, and this time there was no way he could manage the situation. His life was literally in another man's hands.

The boys had kissed him goodbye, and he had the newest animal drawing from Toby in his pocket.

"We'll come and visit you every day," Bran had told him.

He wanted to shout at Justin not to let them visit, but he didn't have to. They'd exchanged glances, and Justin nodded his understanding. He would protect Bran and Toby from anything that might hurt them.

All he wanted to do was get in the car and sleep, but there was one thing he'd needed to do first. He just had to be very sure that Justin knew what to do if the surgery went wrong, or the outcome wasn't good. He tugged him to one side and spoke quietly.

"Promise me something, Justin."

Justin looked wary. "What?"

"If this all goes wrong, you have to help me. You have to make sure, however often I ask you…"

"Rob?"

"Don't give me the gun, never again, and don't let me end it all. Help me fight."

Justin's wary expression vanished, and he gripped Rob's hand. "Always."

That done, Rob relaxed a little, and when Aaron called him to go to the car, Rob felt at peace.

Whatever happened, happened. Wasn't that how it went?

AND NOW THEY WERE HERE, at the hospital, and in less than twenty-four hours he would know what was going to be left of him. He had a DNR set up, no heroic measures to keep him alive on a ventilator. If things went wrong, then he wanted to slip away because he couldn't imagine the hell for

Bran and Toby visiting him if he was in a coma or awake but unable to communicate.

"Ready?" Aaron asked after they'd sat in the car in the parking lot for a good fifteen minutes. Aaron had sensed he needed time to psyche himself up, simply held his hand tight, and waited.

Rob closed his burning eyes, finding it hard to swallow through the tightness in his throat, and nodded. "Yeah."

***

WHEN HE WOKE FROM SURGERY, the fire in his veins was like acid that burned so hot he wanted to die. Then the meds kicked in, and everything was fluffy clouds and soft water.

And through it all, Aaron's voice or Bran's or Toby's always anchored him.

***

HE COULD WALK. Slowly, shakily, and dosed up to the eyeballs with medication, he actually walked. He couldn't tell if the pain in his arms was still there, because everything hurt.

Everything.

Intravenous broad-spectrum antibiotic therapy lasted ten days, and by the end of it, with Aaron supporting his weight, he managed to use the bathroom on his own. Something about Aaron holding his head as he was sick and pissing all at the same time, made Rob's heart hurt. He didn't want to be pathetic.

"Did you know I once single-handedly took down four members of a cell in Seattle, that were running drugs and guns across the border to finance bomb making in the city?" He said, as he clutched the toilet and Aaron's hand.

"You never told me that, no."

"I did. All on my own."

Not like the pathetic thing he'd become.

"I want to hear all about it. Tomorrow. When you wake up."

THE FIRST DAY back at Crooked Tree, after a total of three weeks in the hospital, with swelling pressing on his spine, he cried in Aaron's arms.

The second day, he got angry, shouting at Aaron and scaring the boys.

The third when Bran brought him tiny pieces of a cut-up grilled cheese sandwich, he was told categorically that he'd scared Toby yesterday.

Even though the pain was like knives in his back, he apologized for shouting.

One the fourth day when Toby finally came back in the room, holding a donut with the chocolate melting on his fingers, he accepted Rob's apology. And Rob accepted the donut.

But it was exactly ten days before he could get up and about for real. He had a walker to shuffle about with, but he managed a reasonable distance in circles around the sofa. The boys were watching cartoons and simply peered around him every time he walked in front of them.

This was normal.

I love normal.

WHEN THREE MONTHS HAD PASSED, and the hospital

gave him the post-op all clear, he and Aaron celebrated with Bran and Toby. Sam made a cake. There were mocktails, cupcakes, so much food that it would never be finished, and through it all, Aaron was at his side.

Darkness claimed the ranch, and Bran and Toby had fallen asleep a long time ago, tired from running, and laughing so hard that it had been contagious. Aaron and Rob went to sit on the porch, staring up at the stars, sipping on some nonalcoholic mix of orange and cranberry, complete with small umbrellas, chatting, talking about the party.

"I love you," Aaron said.

He'd spoken clearly and firmly as if he was expecting Rob to disagree with him or tell him that he was stupid.

"Aaron—"

"I spoke to Eddie. He has a friend, Zach, who does building work, and he'd quoted me for extending the house. He could have it done in four months or so, quicker if my brothers help me on our off days."

"Aaron—"

"And the boys could have their own rooms, with a shared bathroom, and there'd be an extra room for someone staying, or if we decided to adopt—"

Rob stopped him from talking by pressing a finger to his lips.

He had just one thing to say under the star strewn night sky.

"I love you, too."

Epilogue

THE CROOKED TREE BARBECUE WAS IN FULL SWING BY THE time Rob made it there. He'd taken a job at the hospital he'd been treated in, in charge of security strategy, and it was coming up on his two year anniversary of joining them. The board told him they'd never felt so safe, probably because he ran the security with a grip of steel and didn't hesitate to do what it took to keep everyone safe.

Somewhere along the way, he'd realized that this was what he was good at; ensuring other people's lives weren't at risk.

He'd approached them directly, wanting something real to work on, and he and the boys had moved into Aaron's place in town, extending it enough so the boys had their own rooms. Bran and Toby slept in the same bed for the first month, but after that, they began to enjoy their individual space. Neither of them scared that anyone would hurt them or separate them. Both of them at the local school and thriving.

Toby loved reading, and that was something Rob could help him with. They'd moved on from teddies in the attic, and he was rereading *Narnia* out loud to his nephew every night.

They were reading *Prince Caspian* right now, but both agreed that *The Magician's Nephew* was the best one.

Bran was heavily into football and had all the moves. Rob couldn't work on tackling with him, limited to catching and throwing long, but he did his bit. He also laughed at Aaron when his lover ended up on the ground with Bran on his chest holding the ball and yelling in victory.

And now Aaron was waiting for him in the parking area, impatient, smiling and hugging him hard.

"You made it!" he said and began to tug Rob over the bridge to Branches. Justin was in charge of the barbecue, much to Sam's horror, but it all seemed good so far. He stopped halfway across the bridge, a sudden memory of him and the boys sitting under the tree talking about Suzi. Aaron stopped tugging him and instead rounded on him immediately.

"Are you okay?"

Rob laughed. That was the same old question, and Aaron never stopped asking it.

"I'm fine," he said. "No pain, no headache, no nothing. Stop worrying."

Aaron cupped his face. "I'll never stop asking if you're okay, you know."

He'd been one of the lucky ones. He'd survived the operation, hadn't lost much feeling, although some days he had to resort to a stick for walking. But the headaches were gone, his memory clear, and he had a whole new life now.

Another car arrived in the parking area, and they glanced back to see Saul and Grace along with Louis, now a toddler who'd flourished with the adoration of two people who loved each other so much.

He and Aaron didn't have long alone now. He knew he'd want to hold Louis, talk some more about maybe extending their family, adopting a kid who was as lost as Toby and Bran had been. He felt so good, invincible, with his whole life in front of him. He just had one thing to do now before they joined Luke's birthday barbecue.

Rob lifted a hand to cover Aaron's on his face, then turned to press a kiss to Aaron's palm.

"I think the next celebration here should be for our wedding," he said.

Aaron blinked at him. "Our wedding?"

"Aaron, I love you so much. Me, you, the boys, we're a family, so let's do this. Will you marry me?"

Then they kissed, and Aaron was laughing, and in the middle of all of that, he was saying yes, over and over.

Rob knew one thing. He should never have thought to give up on life. Not when he had all of this.

Hand in hand they walked up to the barbecue. Toby and Bran ran to them, hugging Rob. They had stories to tell him. Bran had caught a really high ball Luke had thrown him. Toby had drawn an elephant. Normal stuff.

Real life.

Family.

THE END

Also by RJ Scott

The Texas Series

The Heart Of Texas, Texas Book 1

Riley Hayes, the playboy of the Hayes family, is a young man who seems to have it all: money, a career he loves, and his pick of beautiful women. His father, CEO of HayesOil, passes control of the corporation to his two sons; but a stipulation is attached to Riley's portion. Concerned about Riley's lack of maturity, his father requires that Riley *'marry and stay married for one year to someone he loves'*.

Angered by the requirement, Riley seeks a means of bypassing his father's stipulation. Blackmailing Jack Campbell into marrying him "for love" suits Riley's purpose. There is no mention in his father's documents that the marriage had to be with a woman and Jack Campbell is the son of Riley Senior's arch rival. Win win.

Riley marries Jack and abruptly his entire world is turned inside out. Riley hadn't counted on the fact that Jack Campbell, quiet and unassuming rancher, is a force of nature in his own right.

This is a story of murder, deceit, the struggle for power, lust and love, the sprawling life of a rancher and the whirlwind existence of a playboy. But under and through it all, as Riley learns over the months, this is a tale about family and everything that that word means.

Complete Series

The Heart Of Texas

Texas Winter

Texas Heat

Texas Family

Texas Christmas

Texas Fall

Texas Wedding

Texas Gift

RJ Scott - have you read?

Bodyguards Inc series

A mix of family, friends, danger and sexy bodyguards.

- Book 1 – Bodyguard to a Sex God
- Book 2 – The Ex Factor
- Book 3 – Max and the Prince
- Book 4 – Undercover Lovers
- Book 5 – Love's Design
- Book 6 – Kissing Alex

The Heroes series

A series of three books featuring a SEAL, a Marine and a Cop, and the guys that fall for them…

- A Reason To Stay - Book 1
- Last Marine Standing - Book 2
- Deacons Law - Book 3

Meet RJ Scott

RJ is the author of the over one hundred published novels and discovered romance in books at a very young age. She realized that if there wasn't romance on the page, she could create it in her head, and is a lifelong writer.

She lives and works out of her home in the beautiful English countryside, spends her spare time reading, watching films, and enjoying time with her family.

The last time she had a week's break from writing she didn't like it one little bit and has yet to meet a bottle of wine she couldn't defeat.

www.rjscott.co.uk | rj@rjscott.co.uk

NEWSLETTER

Tumblr | Facebook Group | Full Book List

f facebook.com/author.rjscott

🐦 twitter.com/Rjscott_author

📷 instagram.com/rjscott_author

BB bookbub.com/authors/rj-scott

𝓟 pinterest.com/rjscottauthor

Made in the USA
Middletown, DE
27 December 2018